Saturday Night Cleaver

A Barbara Marr Murder Mystery

SATURDAY NIGHT CLEAVER

A BARBARA MARR MURDER MYSTERY

KAREN CANTWELL

CHAPTER ONE

I blame the Internet.

After suffering three straight days of crushing fatigue, I decided to do a little research. Unfortunately, that research eventually led me to a page listing thirty-four symptoms of menopause. Number four on that list was fatigue.

Sitting in my cramped and cluttered closet-turned-office, with a cup of coffee warming my left hand, I clicked the arrow on my computer keyboard to scroll down the checklist.

Hmm.

Hot flashes? Yes, I'd had a few.

Irregular periods? Several of my recent cycles had not been so regular.

Mood swings? Definitely. Happy one minute, crying the next. Just ask my kids. Also my husband, the cats, the dog, the mailman, and that annoyingly slow teller at the bank.

Hair loss? As a matter of fact, I'd just discovered the beginning of a bald patch and blamed my new coconut oil shampoo.

Headaches? Yes.

Dizziness? Yes.

Bloating? Yes.

Bleeding gums? Yes.

Panic disorder? YES! I was panicking at that very moment.

There were other symptoms which I won't describe because they were, um...personal, but suffice it to say of the thirty-four symptoms of menopause listed on that page, I had all thirty-four of them.

1

To calm myself down I took a deep cleansing breath followed by a hefty swig of the coffee. Well, I thought, no need to worry. There was a treatment. I typed "Hormone Replacement Therapy" into the search engine. I'd heard this term bandied about on shows like Oprah and The View. Not that those women were shining examples of successful therapies. If Congress ever felt the need to pass a bill requiring the incarceration of all menopausal women, and wanted the country's support, all they needed to do was tell everyone to tune into The View. Those are some moody, moody ladies.

In any event, I didn't have to dig too deep to find out that the hormones for Hormone Replacement Therapy are derived from horse urine. That was a disturbing fact. I'm not a horse. The idea of taking pills that were in any possible way connected to horse pee gave me a serious case of skin-crawling heebie jeebies.

So that's how I found Dr. Sadistic.

I mean, Dr. Sadjik.

Dr. Sadjik was a holistic physician I sought out at the Natural Life Wellness Clinic on the north side of Rustic Woods. She was forcing me to become a healthier person through diet and exercise. Well, okay she wasn't forcing me, but she did exert a good amount of force by pushing the guilt button. You know, things like, "Your body is a temple to be worshiped, not corrupted," and "Don't you want to live long enough to see your grandchildren?" Things like that. Okay, I'm making that up. She actually didn't push any button of guilt. But she did sit there with that taut, glowing skin, looking at me through clear, bright eyes, as if she were plucked from a granola ad (I think I even heard angels singing), and I knew that I had to follow her plan.

A healthy diet filled with fresh, organic fruits, vegetables, beans, nuts, seeds, fish, and chicken, plus a daily elephant-sized dose of supplements, topped off by an hour of exercise a day, would bring my body into proper balance and the symptoms of menopause should minimize. At first, this didn't seem so bad. I can do that, I thought.

But then she handed me a list of foods I couldn't eat.

Stupid Internet.

No sugar, white flour, egg yolks, white rice, red meat, white pota-
toes, processed foods of any sort, chips, sodas, fried foods, cakes, cook-
ies, donuts, candy. Basically: everything I enjoyed eating.

Maybe the horse-pee pills weren't such a bad idea after all. I mean,
people are always saying, "So-and-so is as healthy as a horse," and
health was what I was going for.

As I was leaving the office with a fifty-page volume of things I
couldn't eat, and a very short list of things I could, Dr. Sadistic, I mean
Dr. Sadjik, reminded me: "And don't forget to exercise for an hour
each day."

I stared at her blankly, wondering how I would possibly have any
energy for exercise on her despotic diet of lettuce and bean sprouts.

So, on a chilly November morning three days after beginning
Mission: Slay Menopause, I tied myself into a pair of sneakers and
prepared for a brisk one-hour walk. The crushing fatigue had not
diminished entirely, so the shoelace-tying alone, was not an easy task
to confront. A few months earlier, I would have talked my friend and
next door neighbor, Roz Walker, into keeping me company, but one
too many "adventures" involving guns and felons had scared her and
her family clear across the continent. When the deal to sell their house
fell through in the eleventh hour, they found a young, childless couple
to rent it at the last minute. I'd spoken with our new neighbors only a
few times, so I hadn't yet graduated to a come-on-a-walk-with-me level
of acquaintance.

But I had other friends to employ. My tummy grumbled as I dialed
Peggy's number, hoping she'd agree to join me on my jaunt. She must
have seen my name on caller ID. "Ciao, Signora!" she answered perk-
ily. "Come stai?"

Peggy Rubenstein was my good friend whose Irish genetic code
was apparent in her fiery red hair and pasty white skin. She grew up on
corned beef, cabbage, and soda bread, and then, at the age of twenty-
five, fell deeply in love with the very Jewish Simon Rubenstein. She said
good-bye to the Pope and hello to Rabbi Goldman. But, when the new-
lywed Rubensteins landed on the shores of Bella Italia while honey-
mooning, Peggy found her true calling: the religion of Italianism. She

fell in love with the people and the culture. Ever since, she's walked Italian, talked Italian, cooked Italian, and often forgotten that her maiden name was McCarthy and not Minelli. Because I'd known Peggy for so long, I knew that "Come stai?" was Italian for "How are you?"

"I've been better," I said, "but it's nothing that an hour-long, invigorating walk won't cure. Wanna come?"

"I would, Bella, but there's a Fall Festival planning meeting at Dandi Booker's house."

Ugh. Dandi Booker. She was the new PTA president at Tulip Tree Elementary. Dandi was possibly the shortest woman I'd ever met, but what she lacked in height she made up for in zippy enthusiasm. She was like a high school cheerleader on a caffeine drip. You know: one of those people who just *loves* everybody. I don't trust people who *love* everybody. It's not natural. You have to dislike some people and I'm not just talking about Hitler and puppy killers. For that reason, I was wary of Dandi Booker. Peggy claimed I was paranoid and that Dandi was just the nicest person and I needed to give her a chance. For that reason, I was starting to hate Dandi Booker. Peggy was *my* friend first and I was beginning to suspect that Dandi was stealing her away. Roz had already deserted me, so losing Peggy was out of the question.

"Forget Dandi," I said, reining in the urge to whine. "Play hooky. Please, please, please."

"I can't, she needs my pumpkins."

"Sounds like a bad pick-up line to me."

I heard her sigh. "Another day, but I gotta run now."

"Some friend you are."

"This diet is making you very grumpy. Is there hope you'll feel better soon?"

"Walking and talking with a good friend is just the medicine I need for the grumpies. Tell Dandi she can have your pumpkins later. And while you're at it, would you ask her how she got that silly name?"

"I'll call you later. Maybe we can get together for a glass of wine."

"It's not allowed."

"Coffee?"

"Nope."

"Green tea, then."

"Have you tasted green tea? You might as well throw three blades of grass in a cup of hot water and call it healthy, because that's what green tea tastes like." The urge to complain had grown stronger than my ability to hold it at bay.

"Barb?"

"Yeah?"

"I love you, and I know the last few months have been really rough on you, but I need to go right now. I'll call you later, okay?"

"Yeah."

A dial tone buzzed in my ear. I clicked the receiver off and contemplated my options. Husband Howard couldn't walk that fast, that far, or that long with his bad leg. Daughters Bethany and Amber had just left for a fun-filled day of education at Tulip Tree Elementary School, and teenaged Callie had zipped off to Rustic Woods High in Howard's Camry. I sighed, then clicked the phone back on and hit number three on my speed dial. "Pick up, pick up, pick up," I murmured under my breath.

After four rings, my body relaxed when a familiar voice answered. "Yo."

"I need you."

"Tell me something I don't know, Beautiful."

Speed dial number three was my buddy from the college days, Colt Baron, who had been kind enough to walk with me the day before. Colt was confident, sexy, and sensitive all at the same time. He had wispy blond hair barely touched by gray, a good view from behind when he wore jeans, an enviable talent for cooking, and he really needed a woman in his life to pamper. I'd been working on finding him the right woman, but for today, was hoping he'd be willing to pamper me. Or at least keep me company.

"Walk with me again today?"

"I told you yesterday, I can't. I'm on a job."

Did I mention that Colt's a private investigator? Adds to the whole sexy-factor.

"Start after the walk," I said.

"Curly, I'd walk with you to the Moon any other day of the week, but today is a no-go. Out of the question. How about your mother?"

"I'd rather walk with Mussolini," I said with an uncontrollable grimace.

"Mama Marr?"

Alka Marr was Howard's mother who lived with us and who was known to just about everyone as Mama Marr. "Her sciatica is acting up." My grimace had turned into a pout. I decided to play the guilt card. "After Howard's accident you said that you were here for me whenever I needed you, and I need you now."

"That was three months ago and I was there for you twenty-four hours a day, seven days a week, remember? I turned down job after job to be with you and the girls. I need to make some money now before the bill collectors start camping out on my front door."

Hmm. That backfired. Now I was the one that felt guilty. "You sure know how to make a girl feel bad."

"That's not what I meant to do." Another call must have beeped through on his line because his voice cut out briefly. "Curly—gotta take this call. Listen, I'll stop by tonight and fix you guys my famous tacos."

"No red meat."

"Chicken tacos."

Colt Baron chicken tacos. I'd take those. "Okay. Have fun making money."

"I plan on it. Love ya."

"Yeah, yeah." Everyone was full of love for me today, but not enough to make them drop their plans and hit the trails.

"Hey, quick question," he said. "Those new neighbors of yours, the Penobscotts. Did I see white rocks in their front yard? The decorative kind? Landscaping rocks."

"Where Roz used to live? They did a little re-landscaping when they moved in, but I'll be honest, I haven't looked that closely. Why?"

"No reason. See you tonight."

For the second time in just five minutes, a dial tone buzzed in my lonely ears.

"Double poo," I shouted to no one in particular. Puddles the poodle, who had been lounging on the rug in front of the sliding-glass door, raised his head and yapped twice at my outburst.

"No backtalk from you, Mister Man," I snapped. "It looks like you're going to be my walking companion today, so get used to it."

"I'll go with you."

I turned to see Howard limping down the hallway, a cane in his left hand, a book in his right, and three days worth of beard growing on that face that made my heart melt. He looked a little like George Clooney—same dark, gray-streaked hair, a little less chin, slightly softer features. I had to admit, he was supremely handsome as husbands go.

"You," I replied sternly while stepping forward to help him, "are going nowhere except to the couch to rest that leg like the doctor ordered. You're going to do what he says so I can have my happy, healthy husband back and life can get back to normal around here. No more hospitals, no more surgeries. You hear me?"

He shook off my attempt to assist him. "I'm tired of sitting on the couch and I'm not an invalid. The doctor said to rest the leg regularly, not to immobilize it. Walking around does me good."

He was right. I was probably overreacting. "Someone is moody," I teased. "Are you going through menopause too?"

Howard frowned, obviously neither pleased nor affected by my attempted levity. Three months earlier, during his last day on the job as an agent with the Federal Bureau of Investigations, Howard's SUV took a five-roll tumble, narrowly missing a dive off the overpass and onto Interstate 66 below. I know, because I witnessed the entire metal-crunching, heart-stopping episode while teaching Callie to drive home from a dentist appointment. If I hadn't been an eyewitness, I would probably have never known what really occurred. As it was, no one, not Howard, nor one person at the Bureau would tell me who they were escorting that day or why that car came out of nowhere firing endless rounds of lead at the government vehicles.

Of the five agents involved, only one lost his life. Howard was touch and go since he'd unbuckled to warn civilian vehicles on the road to stop approaching the mission gone dangerously wrong. He'd spent a week on life support in a doctor-induced coma which allowed his brain to heal from the head trauma. They didn't let him come home until two weeks after he'd regained consciousness. Even then the damage to his left leg and collar bone were so extensive that he went back to the hospital for three additional surgeries.

To say that he'd experienced emotional ups and downs would be the biggest understatement since the crew of Apollo 13 told Houston they had a problem. And unfortunately, the downs seemed way deeper than the ups seemed high. However, I have learned the hard way that when you see the love of your life come excruciatingly close to death, patience becomes as easy and natural as breathing. This current little display of irritation was nothing a bit of TLC couldn't fix.

"My walks are an hour long, but I'll tell you what—you can walk Puddles and me up to the path." I placed a warm kiss on his scruffy cheek. "Deal?"

He emitted a low grumble that I interpreted as an affirmative.

I tugged a fleece jacket from a hanger in the hall closet, slipped a pair of mittens into one pocket, three grocery bags for collecting doggy poop into the other, and snapped the leash onto Puddles' collar. We were one week into a startlingly chilly Virginia November so I decided to grab my fluffy, warm scarf too, just in case. Those woods could get pretty nippy, even if I paced myself at a good clip.

One of the beauties of our quaint Northern Virginia suburb, is the fifty five miles of paved walking paths that run throughout the forested community. A person can get exercise and commune with nature simultaneously. Admittedly, I hadn't really availed myself of the benefit in the six years we'd lived there, but I was developing new respect and admiration for it now.

Technically, the walking path I traversed wound along behind my house, but a person would have to trudge through some dense woods and briar bushes then, if nimble, climb down a long and steep incline to arrive there. The neighborhoods in Rustic Woods aren't like typical cookie cutter suburban sprawls, hence, the name. Houses sit on three-quarter more acre lots that are usually heavily wooded on the backend.

I always opted for the easier route to the walking path—a thin, mulched trail that ran from White Willow Lane along the edge of the Perkin's property. Mr. and Mrs. Perkins lived on just the other side of our neighbors the Penobscotts who Colt had mentioned. Howard walked me from our driveway to the mulched trail. As we passed the Penobscotts' house, I noticed something interesting.

"Well I'll be," I said.

Howard peeked around me. "What are you looking at?"

"White rocks in that flower bed."

"Against policy?" He was referring to the rigid rules set forth by the illustrious and ever-enforcing Rustic Woods Home Owners Association. Rules and regulations that kept most residents quaking in their boots, wondering if a hefty fine was waiting in their near future for something as simple as painting their door the wrong color or installing an outdoor light fixture that didn't match the style of the house.

I shook my head. "Colt just asked me if the Penobscotts used white rocks when they re-landscaped."

"Really?"

"He's way more observant than I give him credit for," I said.

"He has to be, it's how he makes his living."

"But why would that interest him?"

"Heck if I know."

We'd reached the mulched trail. He kissed me sweetly on the lips. His were warm and soft and made me want to run with him back to the house for some long and passionate morning delight. That would be exercise, right? Except we hadn't been doing a whole lot of that since the accident. In fact, we'd done a whole lot of *none* of that since the accident, which, trust me, was completely out of character for my usually-horny hubby. Heck, two hours after his vasectomy, with his family jewels swollen to the size of cantaloupes, he was practically begging for some nookie time. Any attempt on my part, though, to discuss his recent lack of interest, was immediately shut down by him. Attributing the issue to post-traumatic stress, I tried to be understanding and wait things out, but despite the fact that "low sex drive" was one of my thirty-four symptoms of menopause, my desire hadn't ceased to exist entirely.

"Do you have your cell phone?" he asked.

I nodded, thinking more about how I wanted another kiss. "And my mace." I patted the pocket that also held the grocery bags just to be sure I could still feel it there. Check. If Puddles' glass-shattering yips and yaps didn't scare a would-be attacker, a handy shot of pepper spray would.

As Howard limped his way back home, I strode the twenty or so paces to the macadam-paved walking path. Once there, I had the choice of turning to my left or to my right. The previous two days, I had gone right. Today, for some strange reason—let's call it pathetically bad luck—I decided to go left instead. The paths were long and winding, much like that road in the Beatles song, so my strategy was to walk for thirty minutes, then turn around and walk back, giving me the prescribed one hour. Two minutes into the regimen, I realized why I hadn't brought the dog along before. It's very hard to get any momentum and heart rate up when your companion needs to sniff everything in sight and then pee on it for good measure. Thank goodness humans don't mark their territory the way dogs do, or we'd be living in a very, very wet and smelly world.

The air temperature seemed to be going down rather than up. I could see my breath now, and even the mittens, which I had eventually resorted to, didn't keep the bite away. I tugged at Puddles a few more times in an attempt to pick up some speed and warm up, but I was losing interest real fast. My watch told me we'd been at it for fifteen minutes and I was about ready to call it quits when Puddles started barking wildly at a pile of leaves beside a rotting tree trunk. His nose was inches from the pile and as he managed to pull himself closer, he barked even louder.

Who knew what was under that pile. I assumed a dead animal—a squirrel maybe—but didn't really want to find out, so I bent down to lift Puddles up with the intention of carrying him back home. As it turned out, that was the wrong thing to do, because too much slack went into his leash. With the ferocity of a lion after a kill, Puddles dove headfirst into the pile and sent leaves spraying.

"Puddles!" I hollered, heading back in for another attempt to scoop him up. In the process, my foot landed on something that squished, then cracked. If it had just cracked, I would have thought 'twig'. It was the squish that caused me to step away and look closer.

After brushing a few damp leaves away, I gagged instinctively. Four dirty fingers, one thumb. Gray fingernails. Chopped at the wrist.

Meanwhile, Puddles was going to town on that pile of leaves.

Having just stepped on a human hand that did not have a body attached, my mind reeled at what the dog might have discovered. I yanked hard on the leash, not even caring about poor Puddles' neck. He barely noticed. He just growled and shook the prize in his mouth like it was his chewy toy at home. In fact, when I focused more closely, it kind of looked like his chewy toy. The one that's shaped like a sausage but squeaks like a lab rat on mind-altering drugs.

I was still working to hold back the strong impulse to unload my morning's portion of organic, honey-sweetened oatmeal when I realized what Puddles had discovered.

That friends, was another body part.

A *male-only* body part, if you catch my drift.

And unfortunately, even if the male to whom it had once belonged was alive and could get it back, he'd probably say, "No thanks," since Puddles was...how should I put this? Finding it awfully tasty.

Welcome to the world of Barbara Marr. I'm a wife, friend, daughter, mother-of-three, and apparently, I'm unusually prone to stumbling upon the messy remnants of lurid crime scenes.

CHAPTER TWO

Ultimately, I didn't throw up. I didn't scream either. I didn't even cry. In fact, I dialed 911 with an amazing and almost eerie sense of calm. Once I separated Puddles from his morning snack, that is.

Grisly discoveries had become far too common lately. Was it me, or was it Rustic Woods? Maybe I should have followed Roz's example and hightailed it out of town months ago. Of course, that was all twenty-twenty hindsight sort of thinking, since I was now sitting in the back of a police cruiser wrapped in a blanket and sipping a hot cup of coffee thanks to my friend who I liked to call Officer Brad.

Officer Brad's real name was Eric Lamon. Or Officer Lamon, to those who hadn't had the intimate experience (like me) of jointly bringing down a ring of misfit Mafia goons who'd been dealing in pharmaceuticals. Really. It happened. In any event, Eric looks a whole lot like Brad Pitt, thus the nickname. When he became a good friend of the family, however, I resorted to addressing him by his given name—it's easier and less embarrassing for both of us. He's one hunk of policeman, let me tell you. And a nice guy to boot. Not every cop would run out and get a cup of coffee for a freezing woman who'd just uncovered a man's pogo-stick in a pile of leaves.

Eric stood talking with three other uniformed, gun-toting law-men. Several others, many of them gloved and masked, climbed in and out of the woods. The flashing blue and red lights had attracted a gaggle of neck-craning onlookers.

When his conversation ended, the handsome policeman strode my way. "How's the coffee?"

Yes, I had broken down, dismissed Dr. Sadistic's list of forbidden beverages, and savored that steamy cup of java like a smoker two hours late for cigarette break. "Perfect," I said with a smile. The cool air made my warm breath visible. "Nothing like roasted blend after a brisk morning walk and close encounters of the revolting kind."

He chuckled, but turned back to business. "We have everything we need from you now. Do you need a ride home?"

"Howard is on his way."

"How is he doing?" When word got to Eric about Howard's accident, he had been extraordinarily helpful to all of us, but mostly to Howard.

"Walking with a cane and generally better overall." I sneaked a sip of my brew, then added, "A little grumpy sometimes."

"You can expect that for a while. A buddy of mine took a bullet in the spine during a routine traffic stop. He was not a nice guy until he decided to turn over a new leaf and found a different job."

Puddles was beside me on the seat barking, panting, and going all dog-crazy. I rubbed his head to calm him down. "What's your friend doing now?"

"He's a barista at Cappuccino Corner. Brewed that cup you're drinking."

"He's happy?"

"Happiest I've ever seen him, actually."

My phone jingled in my hip pack. I pulled it out, expecting to see Howard's name on the ID, but saw Peggy's instead. I took the call.

"Did you give Dandi your pumpkins?" I asked, bypassing the traditional "hello."

"Marla Hepple just showed up and said that Sweet Birch Road is crawling with emergency vehicles. I figured you must be in trouble."

I felt irrationally peeved that flashing squad car lights in Rustic Woods were taken as evidence of another Barbara Marr commotion.

"I'm not in trouble." This, I would argue, was not a lie.

"Are you sure?"

"Positive. I'm just warming myself up with a cup of coffee after my walk."

"Coffee? I thought that wasn't allowed on your diet."

Just then, the police radio crackled and a dispatcher's voice squawked something in code. I cringed.

"I heard that!" Peggy shouted. "You're in a police car, aren't you?"

Dropping the happy-go-lucky act, I laid into her. "It's all your fault. If you'd come with me, I wouldn't have brought the dog. So when you read about this in the paper, just remember, you're the reason why."

"What happened?"

"No way, Jose. I'm not telling you with half the Tulip Tree Elementary Rumor Brigade listening in."

"Are you okay? Should I come over?"

Her offer tempered my mood. "You'd do that? What about Dandi and your pumpkins?"

"Boy, you're not going to let that go, are you?"

I spotted my white Grand Caravan pulling behind the cruiser. "Howard's pulling up now. We'll probably be home in five minutes or so."

"See you soon." She clicked off.

My husband, ever the FBI agent, hung around for several minutes talking to Officer Lamon and his associates. No one seemed to mind that he no longer carried a badge. I didn't dare complain that I was cold and wanted to go home because he looked more engaged than I'd seen him in months. Even resting on the cane, you could tell he was back in his element. Howard, I thought, would never be happy brewing coffee and chai lattes.

"So," Howard said suppressing a smirk as he buckled in for our drive home. "You can't just pick up discarded soda cups and water bottles like normal people?"

"It wasn't me, it was your dog."

His mouth tugged into a playful grin. "Now he's *my* dog?"

"Hey buddy, I'll admit I've grown to tolerate, and maybe even care a little for that yappy mutt, but he's always been *your* dog. It's bad enough that his yowling can give a banshee nightmares, now he thinks he's a bloodhound."

He looked both ways for traffic, then made a U-turn to head back home. "Lamon said he'd keep us informed when they learn more about the victim."

"No!" The shout that escaped my mouth surprised even me. "I don't want to be informed. I want to remain blissfully ignorant. Like that chubby guy in Hogan's Heroes. You got it?"

He smiled. "You aren't even curious? Not everyone finds a pe-"

I put my hand in front of his mouth, preventing the "p" word from escaping before it hurt my ears. "Don't say it. You know I hate that word."

It's true. There are a few words in the English language that affect me like fingernails on a blackboard, and the moniker for a male member is one of them. Others include booger, kumquat (don't ask me why), and when George W. Bush says "nuc-u-ler" instead of "nuc-lee-er."

I'm not a prude, don't get me wrong. I have no issue with the actual item itself, just the name. It probably stems from an experience with sex education when my mother decided to relay the story of the birds and the bees. Only, she didn't call them the birds and the bees, she called them "Mother" and "Father" and provided a very graphic slide show presentation to assist me achieve perfect understanding. They weren't home pictures or anything like that—my mother considered herself progressive, but not *that* progressive. No, these were detailed drawings of both male and female organs as well as images of the act itself, all provided by the kit she had purchased, "Talk Sex Now, Avoid Pregnancy Later." The problem was, I was only three years old, and I'm pretty sure the kit was intended for presentation to children ten or older. At the time, I thought she referred to that dangly thing hanging on the daddy as a "peanut." Well one day, while sitting in the waiting room of a doctor's office, a young boy near me kept pulling at his pants. It seemed a little odd, so I whispered to my mom, "Why is he grabbing on his peanut?"

My mother became very irritated with me, and huffed loud enough for the entire waiting room of patients as well as the world to hear, "It's a pee-*nis*, Barbara." She emphasized the NIS. "Pee-*nis*. I've told you before. That little boy is grabbing on his pee-*nis*."

Just retelling the horror story causes me to feel faint and I can only imagine the therapy that little boy has had to endure later in life.

I've adopted the Swahili word *uume*—pronounced oo-may. I find it much more appealing, thank you very much. And a little more masculine, quite frankly. You know, sort of like, "Oh, my."

"What's the word we use?" I reminded him.

He shook his head and I detected the genesis of an eye roll, but he stopped himself. "I don't remember."

Men, they can't remember anything. "*Uume*. I found an *uume*. There was a hand, too, if you recall. And no, I'm not curious."

"I don't believe that."

"Fine, I'm curious, but that's as far as I'm taking this. No more adventures for me. No Mafia, no bank robbing fugitives, no paranoid, corrupt politicians and their henchmen, and no vengeful wives with sharp kitchen knives bent on dismembering their cheating husbands."

He threw me a look. "Why do you assume it's a cheating husband?"

I covered my ears with my hands. "I'm not listening." I began singing The Star Spangled Banner loudly enough to make my point and didn't stop until we had pulled into our driveway.

In the house, Puddles lapped up every last drop in his water bowl, then crashed in his doggy bed as if he'd just run a marathon. He'd had a pretty exciting morning for a little gray poodle.

As for me, I showered immediately.

Somehow, scrubbing for ten minutes didn't seem to wash away the vivid image of blue, dirt-crusted fingernails or the ravaged male organ. When I returned downstairs, hair dripping wet, I found Peggy and Howard laughing at the kitchen table. This was something new. I hadn't seen him laugh that heartily since July. He might have chuckled here or there, but no genuine laughter, despite my best efforts.

"What's so funny?" I asked, hoping they wouldn't say it was me.

"I was just telling Howard about my step-uncle's third cousin on his mother's side, Joe Junior the Third. He didn't have any hands—I can't remember why. Boating accident, maybe?" She brushed her hand in the air. "Something with propellers, I think. Anyway, he qualified for this experimental hand transplant operation, where they gave him the hands of some guy who had just died in the hospital. He was so excited to have hands that he told the doctors he wanted to meet the family of the man who gave him a normal life again. So when he was being discharged, the doctors introduced him to the donor's parents in a lounge—they'd planned this whole affair with cake and local reporters there and everything. Well, much to his shock and dismay, it turned out they were the parents of his sworn enemy—Hugo." She stopped and reconsidered. "No, it was Hector." That didn't seem to work for her either. She tilted her head in thought. "Harold?...something with an H. Once best friends, but now, even though Hector or Harold was dead, Joe Junior hated him worse than cold grits in January. I don't know what that means, but that's what he always said. And if I remember right, the feud was actually about grits. No, no, it was about mutual fund investments. Well, he was so upset that right there in that lounge in front of the parents, the doctors, the reporters and everyone, he ripped his left hand right off, then stomped on his right hand until it broke clean off."

That was probably Peggy's craziest family story to date. "First," I said, grabbing a mug from the cupboard, "I don't believe anyone could just rip a hand off even if it had just been sewn on. But more importantly, I don't know why it's funny. That's just plain creepy."

"That wasn't the funny part," she explained.

I found it hard to believe there was a humorous ending to this story, but I had to find out anyway. "So what' the funny part?"

"The headline in the local newspaper the next day. It read, 'Joe Junior the Turd Gives Back Hands.'"

Howard and Peggy laughed some more. I did not. The Joe Junior tale still didn't elicit a desire to chortle or even giggle mildly, but then again, my mind still wallowed in the lucid memory of crunching on a disembodied appendage, so I probably wasn't the right person to be judging its hilarity factor.

Mama Marr appeared in the kitchen, crunching a few bones of her own. Since she'd moved in with us a few months back, I had learned to predict her arrival in a room by the decibel level of the snap, crackle, and pop that preceded. When she walked, the woman sounded like a bowl of Rice Krispies that had just been doused with a generous helping of milk.

"I hear that you and The Puddles picked up a *prącia* on your walk," Mama Marr said, fanning herself with a pudgy hand. "I think I am glad for the sciatica this morning!"

Mama Marr always referred to Puddles as "The Puddles," and I was pretty sure *prącia* was Polish for *uume.* I liked it. Much more oomph than the wimpy English counterpart. I added it to my mental list of acceptable synonyms.

Howard's mother creaked and popped her way to the stove and her teapot. "I am making the tea, if anyone wants?"

"Not me, Ma," said Howard.

"I need more of the strong stuff, thank you, Mama," I said. I poured hot coffee into my mug.

Howard eyed me with a cocked brow. "Thought that wasn't on the diet."

"When a woman has to disengage a limp and leaf-covered *prącia* from her growling dog's mouth with her numb fingers, she's allowed to take a day off any diet."

Pushing her chair back from the table, Peggy stood. "Tea sounds wonderful Mrs. Marr, but I have to head out again."

"You just got here," I whined. "I didn't get to tell you about the *prącia.*" I put on a pout.

"Howard told me all about it."

"Forgive me if I say that it's not the same as from the horse's mouth. There are subtleties he could never impart."

She patted my hand. "Can you impart them later? Over a glass of wine, perhaps, since you're diet-free today?"

Could I be mad at my friend for not having time? Of course not. We mothers always had some errand to run. One of Peggy's boys probably needed new reeds for his clarinet, or notebooks for science class. Possibly there was a dental appointment on the schedule. I would not make her feel guilty.

I nodded and sneaked a quick sip from the steamy mug. "Sure, we can talk later. What do you have to do?"

She didn't hesitate. "Goldfish."

"The boys want goldfish now?" I groaned. Poor Peggy had been through a myriad of pets, avoiding the larger, more time consuming and messy puppy issue. They'd had hermit crabs, tree frogs, and three different kinds of lizardy looking things. Sadly, none of them had survived the Rubenstein household, may they rest in pieces. I mean, peace.

She shook her head. "No. I have to go the pet store and handle some quantity confusion with the goldfish Dandi ordered for the Fall Festival."

Could I be mad at my friend for not having the time? I sure could, if Dandi Booker was involved. My blood was starting to boil, but I bit back my bitterness and tried to look calm all the same. "Why in person?"

"Dandi claims she ordered three hundred goldfish but the store swears she ordered three thousand and they want the little guys picked up and paid for today. Can you believe it? She asked me to sweet talk them into understanding it was their mistake plus work them down from three hundred to two hundred since it looks like attendance will be lower than she predicted."

"What's the pet store going to do with twenty-eight hundred goldfish?"

"It's their mistake, not ours."

"Sounds to me like it's Dandi's mistake, not *yours*."

Peggy was already standing and slipping into her heavy wool sweater, unfazed by my obvious jab. "I have half a bottle of some white wine in my fridge. When should I bring it by? Eight?"

I turned to my hubby and asked sweetly, "Howard, will you handle bed-time duty for Amber and Bethany?"

He had checked out of the conversation some time ago, skimming over the Rustic Woods Gazette, but he caught my request and nodded. "Will do, Boss."

"Make it seven-thirty," I said to Peggy as Mama Marr's kettle started to scream.

I figured seven-thirty would be perfect timing after the taco dinner that Colt had promised. He could even join us while I described every horrible detail of my grisly morning romp.

I really wanted those tacos and the wine would be an added bonus. What I didn't know at the time was, I wouldn't be enjoying either. Not that night.

CHAPTER THREE

Peggy and my mother must have passed each other in our driveway. Mere moments after Peg walked out the door, Diane Fenstermacher Pettingford, (aka, Mom) blew in. Most people walk in, stride in, step in. Not my mother—she gusts in like a hurricane. No, make that a tornado. Everything is calm. The trees on the leaves are still as can be. Then whoosh! A tornado flies in from out of nowhere and suddenly everyone is heading for cover, hoping to get to the basement or cellar in time. Where my mother is concerned, I never escape the damaging winds. I guess it's the German in her. She doesn't know how to do anything without using force.

"There are enough police cars crawling along Sweet Birch Road to scare Charles Manson. Barbara, please tell me you weren't involved."

And she always forgets to say, "Hello."

"Good morning, Mom. How are you?"

"Truthfully?"

Actually, I would have preferred a quick lie and a goodbye right then, but I was sure her question was rhetorical. "Give it to us."

She leaned against the counter and began pulling a glove off her hand, one finger at a time. "I signed up for a new art class—An Introduction to the World of Sketching—and I've been so excited about starting, but they just informed me that the class will have to be dropped if enough people don't register. They need two more people."

Uh-oh.

Mama Marr was still putzing around in the kitchen, wiping the counter clean of crumbs. She stopped suddenly. "This sketching, Diane. Is it like the drawing with the pencils? Animals and trees and such?"

"That is exactly what it will be Alka." I detected hope in my mother's eyes.

"I think I would like to be in this sketching class. I think I would like to draw my canary, Pavrotti. You know, so I can have a remembrance of him here, since I miss him so much."

Oh boy.

Pavrotti came with Mama Marr from Philadelphia, but quickly needed relocation after my two cats, Indiana Jones and Mildred Pierce, followed their feline instincts and tried to catch him for a mid-day snack. He currently resided peacefully with my mother in her condo across town, but Mama Marr never missed an opportunity to mourn his absence or his sweet, chirpy singing.

My mother clapped her hands in glee and swooped down upon Mama Marr for a giant bear hug. See, my mother is a very large woman. Tall. Big-boned. Amazonian. When she hugs Mama Marr, a petite, roly-poly Polish lady, images of old vampire movies flash before my mind. You know the ones—where the tall, fanged man in the cape completely consumes the small defenseless damsel, because Mama Marr truly disappears behind my mother the way the damsel disappears behind the cape. I often worry we'll never see poor Mama again after a Diane-embrace.

Thankfully, this time, she did come up for air. I breathed a sigh of relief, only to realize I shouldn't relax just yet, because I was most assuredly next on my mother's hit list for art class registrants.

I decided to stop her at the pass. "No, Mom-"

"I already signed you up, dear." She waved a dismissive hand. "You could use a hobby."

"I don't need a hobby." I spotted Howard trying to make a fast getaway, but I was faster. I pointed. "Take Howard. Howard needs a hobby. He's retired."

From the dining room, he looked back at the cane he'd left behind in his mad, limping dash. "I have a job."

"No you don't."

"Start tomorrow, I didn't tell you?"

"You lie like a rug you liar, you."

Mama Marr was practically giddy. "This will be fun, we three ladies drawing pictures with our pencils."

Mom was already on her way out the door and she wasn't accepting Howard as an exchange student. "I'll pick you both up tomorrow at eleven-thirty. We'll go somewhere fun for lunch first."

What she didn't know – and what I didn't plan to tell her – was that Howard had a doctor's appointment at 11:00. I'd show her.

At 3:20, Howard and I meandered to the bus stop at the end of the street. This was the nice part about having him around—the quiet, family moments. Before the accident, he'd never had time to keep up on all of the girls' news about school, ballet, nature club, and the like. He'd missed so many back-to-school nights and parent conferences that most teachers thought I was a single mother. And honestly, sometimes I felt like one. Now we held hands and chatted quietly while waiting for Amber and Bethany. Life was good.

"What's for dinner?" Howard asked.

"Colt said he'd fix us tacos."

There was a time when that would have set Howard into a seething rage. For years he had despised my friendship with Colt. Understandably, since Colt obviously still carried a bit of a torch for me, but the man had been there for Howard day and night during what we now call "the horrible time." The two of them had found peace as true, stalwart, boon-buds.

"Colt Tacos." Howard nodded approvingly. "Sounds good. Do we have any beer in the house? Gotta have beer with tacos."

"I don't think so. I'm saving myself for the wine Peggy's bringing afterwards." I pulled my cell phone out of my pocket and dialed Colt's number to pin him down on a time.

Howard checked his watch. "I'll go to the store in a little while and get some, anyway. For the dudes."

My call went straight to voicemail. I tried Colt's home phone. Message machine. "Colt Barron, Private Investigator. Leave a message. Stay cool."

I left a message, then redialed his cell and left one there, too. He was probably still working and would get back to us soon enough. The girls would be excited to hear Colt was cooking since my culinary repertoire is small and somewhat lacking in the flavor department. Mama Marr says she doesn't care for "the Mexee-canish food," so she'd probably fix herself a bowl of oatmeal and call it a night.

The bus arrived and our girls jumped from the bottom step. First came Bethany, a spectacled twelve-year-old with shiny, raven hair ponytailed. A bouncy, semi-toothless, orange-haired Amber followed on her heels, and they both ran to Howard for their daily hug. Bethany gave me a less tight, but still full-of-love hug, but Amber stopped in her tracks right in front of me. She placed an indignant hand on her hip.

"Mommy," she said with the seriousness of a president about to declare war, "Darla Hepple says her mommy says that you got in trouble again and the police had to attest you. Are you attested?"

That Marla Hepple. I knew she'd start talking. She could never keep her big mouth shut. I'd pegged her as a spotlight-craver from the first time I met her and she introduced herself: "Hi! My name is Marla, and this is my daughter Darla."

I pulled Amber's backpack from her shoulders. "Now, how would Darla hear such a thing when she was in school all day?"

"Her mommy was volunteering in the cafeteria today."

Boy, the woman got around. Working on the Fall Festival then off to volunteer at the school and simultaneously smear my good name.

"I'm not attested and I'm not arrested either," I said. "And next time you see Darla Hepple you tell her that her mommy..."

Howard cleared his throat. As parents, we'd agreed to set a good example and not talk disparagingly of others.

Amber's eyes remained wide and attentive, awaiting my next words.

"Tell Darla that her mommy is such a kind person for being concerned about me! Wow!" I was probably playing it up too much, but Amber didn't seem to notice. Bethany, on the other hand, was rolling her eyes, a habit she picked up from her father. "Mrs. Hepple—just the nicest." I added, just for that cherry-on-the-top effect.

Callie turned in, driving Howard's car, just as we were entering the house. The Marr family was all in one place, happy and content.

When we hadn't heard back from Colt by five, I tried both of his phones again. His cell suspiciously went straight to voicemail rather than ringing first. He wasn't usually this late responding. I wondered if he'd forgotten the taco deal. I supposed it was possible, but not really typical for Colt. When I expressed some concern, Howard brushed me off. "He probably just forgot."

By six-thirty everyone was grumpy and Colt was still nowhere to be found, so I ran out to Taco Loco for a twelve pack and two burritos. Taco Loco tacos were the best crappy fast food tacos around, but they didn't measure up even the tiniest bit to a Colt mexi-masterpiece. Mama Marr had already consumed her bowl of oatmeal and was asleep in front of the TV in her room when I returned.

By seven-thirty, even Howard remarked on the oddity of Colt's truancy. "Maybe he met a woman," he finally concluded with a shrug.

And of course, seven-thirty marked the time Peggy was to arrive, wine in hand, ear to listen, but was she on my doorstep?

No.

I suspected that my blood pressure was rising dangerously high. At eight-fifty, I grabbed one of those beers from the fridge and gulped it a little too quickly, then called Peggy's home. Simon told me she was at Dandi Booker's house. I didn't leave a message.

I'd been stood up not once, but twice. Was I that easy to forget?

Rather than stew about it, I put my energy into getting Amber and Bethany ready for bed. Bethany was actually pretty self-sufficient since she was a big-time fifth grader now, but Amber still loved her Mommy time and so did I. She bathed and I washed then dried her hair, and rubbed lotion on that incessant dry patch on her back. Afterwards, the three of us compacted ourselves into Amber's bed where I read another chapter of *The Wonderful Wizard of Oz.* Big high-school student Callie didn't join us for story time anymore, and while I understood, it still made me a little sad. The times, they were a changin'.

It was almost ten o'clock on a Friday night by the time I found Howard propped up against the headboard of our bed, clicking away at his laptop. Boy, weren't *we* the party animals?

Falling into place beside him, I fluffed a pillow and released a hefty, life-is-crummy sigh, fully expecting Howard to respond the way a good, caring, and attentive husband should: with sympathy. A simple, "What's wrong, honey? Are you sad?" or "It's okay, your friends are scum, but I still love you. Let me show you the ways ..." would do. I don't ask for much. Usually.

He continued to click away on the keyboard, eyes focused on the bright video screen.

"Hmm..." he finally murmured.

It was the hope of conversation. I jumped on it. "I know. It's been a terrible day."

"I thought I'd heard of this," he said, still glued to the screen. "Supposedly an urban myth, but there's some truth behind it."

"Friends breaking promises? No myth. I live the sad reality," I said, knowing full well that we were on two entirely different topics. I wasn't even sure Howard knew I was sitting next to him. He might have been talking to himself.

"White landscaping rocks and suburban swinger clubs."

Suddenly, my woe-is-me discourse seemed a lot less interesting. "Suburban what-er whats?" I heard him just fine, I just wanted to hear those words again all in a row. They were so juicy and thrill-provoking.

"Suburban swinger clubs. White landscaping rocks are supposedly their signature—tells other swingers they're in the neighborhood."

"You mean, like wife swapping? Didn't that go out with disco and dangerously flammable polyester shirts?"

He shook his head and finally smiled at me. Oh, those deep brown eyes. I get lost in them. Some fires were beginning to ignite and I'm not talking about chimneys or Mount Doom. Yes, I was feeling some Howie lust.

"I remember some talk about this at work after a Texas agent worked on a case down there," he said, completely and utterly without romance. "Some pro-family and morality-concerned groups want the FBI to get involved and shut them down as prostitution rings, but it really doesn't apply and it's not our-" he stopped himself, then corrected, "not *their* jurisdiction."

I wanted to cry at the sadness in his voice. Without the FBI he didn't have a job and he felt he didn't have a purpose. A place to go and a place to be needed every day. I wanted to shout at him, pound his thick skull and remind him that his job and purpose was to be a father, husband, and son. *We* needed him and he was exactly where he needed to be. But the moment didn't call for another lecture. We'd had *that* discussion too many times before. Instead, I concentrated on where this research all began. "So, you think there are swingers' clubs in Rustic Woods, Colt is investigating them, and he thinks our neighbors are involved? Yikes."

"I didn't say that."

Outside, a leaf blower revved into action.

"Speaking of neighbors," I said, getting up to look out the window, why I don't know since it was pitch black and street lights were banned in Rustic Woods. "That's the second night I've heard that noise. I think it's coming from the Penobscotts' backyard. Why would they blow leaves around in the middle of the night?"

Howard cocked an ear and listened for a minute. "I don't think that's a leaf blower."

"Lawn mower?"

He shook his head. "No way. Chain saw maybe."

I looked at the digital display on our bedside alarm clock and plopped back into bed. Ten after ten. "Who saws something this late?"

"Do they both work? Maybe this is the only time for him to get stuff done around the house. Fixing his deck maybe?"

This comment burned the feminist in me. "What? You're so sure it's *him* fixing the deck? How do you know it's not *her* out there sweating over those deck boards?" Truthfully, I don't have a hard-line feminist bone in my body. I'm pretty much middle-of-the-road in all of my philosophies. I was just cranky and looking for a fight. The beauty of this particular moment was that Howard knew this.

"Still mad at Colt and Peggy?"

"They stood me up." I was pouting again, although, I'll admit, even I was getting tired of my pity-party. "I'm more worried about Colt, though. If we don't hear from him tomorrow, I'm going over there. As for Peggy, well, she's a traitor. Plain and simple."

"You don't think you're over-reacting?"

"About Colt or about Peggy?"

"Peggy."

"She bailed on me. For Dandi Booker."

"Did you talk to her and find out why?"

"Do I need to?"

He looked at me over his half-eye reading glasses. "You do this, you know."

"What?"

"Go to the worst conclusion first. Isn't she your friend and don't you always say your friendships mean everything to you?"

"What do you mean, I go to the worst conclusion first?" I did not like his accusatory tone.

He flicked a glance to the ceiling, then back to me. "I remember some episode a year or so ago when you were up in arms because Peggy and Roz were doing things without asking you along. You were so sure you were being excluded from lunches and shopping dates, and you even drove by Peggy's house late one night when you thought Roz was over there without you..."

Howard never seemed to have a good memory for things I considered important, why all of the sudden was his recollection of this embarrassing moment in my life so clear? I had driven by Peggy's house that night with my lights out to avoid detection and totaled Simon's old Ford parked at the curb when I careened into it. It was a black car. I couldn't see it. I had to make up a story on the spot that I was out searching for Indiana Jones and a deer darted into the road causing me to swerve. Howard remembered, because our car insurance went up two hundred dollars a month.

My face flamed from anger and shame. I crossed my arms while working hard on a justification for my actions that would make me feel better.

"It seems to me," he continued on like Buddha or Ghandi, "that if you value friendship the way you *say* you do, you'd...I don't know exactly how to put it. You know—assume your friend's intentions were good. I just always see you going to the worst conclusion first."

I know. He'd said that already.

This was beginning to feel like a scene in *To Kill a Mockingbird* with Howard playing Atticus and me portraying Scout, but without the Alabama drone.

"Gee, why don't you whip up a meme for Facebook and share that one around, Mr. Deep?"

The justifications weren't coming quickly enough so I had resorted to name calling. And when I realized my name calling was really lame, I resorted to the very mature you-do-it-too argument.

"You should talk," I huffed. "How about the way you've treated Colt all of these years? Huh? Do you feel good about that?"

He didn't produce the answer I expected. "No," he said simply. Then he elaborated after an especially effective pause that even the great Gregory Peck would have been proud to have delivered. "I don't feel good about how I treated him at all. One thing nearly dying did was help me put my relationships in perspective."

He kissed me on the forehead and then softly, but shortly on the lips. It was the kind of kiss that says, "I love you and now I'm going to sleep." Evidently his marital relationship perspectively did not require a romp in the hay.

Fine by me, because even if we'd been active in the lovemaking department, I wasn't in the mood after his one-two punch-attack on my character. He might have been right, but I wasn't going to like it.

And yes, I know: perspectively isn't a real word.

CHAPTER FOUR

Thankfully, a good night's sleep can cure just about any foul disposition. Saturday morning found me mostly simpatico with Howard again.

He had agreed to see Dr. Sadistic, I mean Dr. Sadjik, for a discussion of his overall health and the prescription of a superior diet like the one I had abandoned in three days flat. He still needed to see his orthopedist for a final pass on the leg and collar bone, and he'd be visiting the neurologist for an undetermined amount of time because of the head trauma, so you'd think we'd be sick of medical practitioners. But after coming so close to losing him, I was determined to see Howard live a good long time whether he liked it or not.

Off we motored to Natural Life Wellness Clinic after telling Mama Marr, sadly, that I had forgotten this appointment and would not be able to make our first art class together.

She shook her head in disappointment. Creak, pop, snap. "You can not make this appointment for another time?"

"Nope," I said. Which was not a lie. Dr. Sadjik and her husband shared the care of their two young children, so she worked early evenings and held Saturday and some Sunday hours. Her schedule booked out weeks in advance since she was only one of a handful of naturally-oriented physicians in the area.

"Too bad for you. Such fun we would have together."

"Yup. Too bad."

"I will take the notes so you can be prepared next Saturday, okie dokie?"

"Okay," I said, while making a mental note to find something urgent to do next Saturday at 11:30.

For the record, it wasn't an art class with poor creaky, canary-less Mama Marr that put me in a panic. It was an art class with Mama Pushy-Pants Pettingford. Really and truly, because my mother would have been running the show. Telling me my apple was too oval or that my vase looked like it was melting onto my oval apple, or that my pear (was that a pear?) was upside down. I already had a teen-aged daughter at home telling me I was wrong at least fifty times a day, I didn't need any more criticism. And besides, I knew my mother wouldn't boss Mama Marr around, so the two of them would sketch away happily together and never even notice my absence, I was quite sure. There. Phew. Absolution complete.

While I drove us to the clinic, I asked Howard to call Colt again. Unfortunately, this produced the same results as the previous day. Just voicemail at home and on his cell. Something was wrong now, and we both knew it, so after Howard's time with Dr. Sadjik where he walked away with the same bad-food tome as mine (except he could keep drinking coffee, which annoyed me greatly), we made a bee-line for Colt's condo. We did not stop at Go, we did not collect our two hundred dollars.

That little trip didn't solve any mysteries. His prized GTO wasn't in the parking lot. We knocked on his door to no avail and peeked through the sliding glass door as well as his bedroom window, which luckily were easy to access since the condo was on the ground floor. We did not see Colt's dead or comatose body lying on any floor, but we also didn't see a live body in bed or eating lunch at the tiny two-person kitchen table. In retrospect, we both realized that we should have thought to stop at our house for the spare condo key we kept.

As we backed out of our parking space to motor back home, a dark blue sedan pulled in two spots over. An Asian woman in a slick suit and small heels exited the driver's side door. She was pretty. Probably in her mid-to-late thirties.

"Slow down," said Howard. "Let's see where she's going."

It became quickly apparent that where she was going was Colt's condo. Without a moment of a second thought, I threw my gear shift into park and leapt from the van. The lady was knocking on the door when she spotted me. Fear shone in her eyes, which she quickly dropped to the ground as she began hoofing it back to her car.

"Wait!" I shouted. "Are you looking for Colt?" I was following her now. "He's my friend."

"No speak English," she spurted, shaking her head. "No speak English."

"I'm worried about-"

She cut me off. "No English!" Her car door slammed and she peeled out of that parking lot faster than Bill Clinton chasing down a lead on a party full of young and eager interns.

Howard was standing outside of the van when I returned, writing on a piece of paper.

"License plate?" I asked.

He nodded. "I'll ask Lamon to run this for me."

"Is he allowed?"

"Officially, no. Will he do it for us? I'm sure he will."

It was good to know good cops. Especially cops that looked like Brad Pitt.

At home, Howard went straight into the house to call Eric while I stepped down to the mailbox to see what bills and junk mail Mr. USPS had delivered to us that fine autumn day. In the process, I ran into our new neighbor and possible deck-fixer, Melody Penobscott.

"Hi Barb!" she waved as she opened the door to her mailbox. Her face was lit with a mile-wide smile. "How are ya?"

Melody was about my height, but as skinny as a stick. Her dirty-blond hair was always pulled back in a ponytail that bounced around as if it were its own entity. It was kind of creepy, that ponytail. I never asked her how old she was but she looked like she was fifteen pretending to be thirty. She and her husband, Neil, moved to the area from Wisconsin and that was about all I knew about them. Oh, and she liked sushi.

They had moved in right after Howard's accident, so I hadn't really had the time or energy to venture into making-friends-with-neighbors territory. Colt had actually talked to them more than I had. I did like our short meet-in-the-street chats though, because she sounded just like Frances McDormand's character in *Fargo*, dontcha know? She said my name Bea-rb, kind of like she was about to say Bear, but then changed her mind at the last minute and changed it up to get that "arb" at the end.

"I'm good," I said, returning her smile but with a little less enthusiasm. "How are you?" I waited, anticipating with relish the response which I knew would be filled with Canadian sounding O's and lots of nasally other vowels.

"Oh, ya know, things are just grand. We love our new house ya know."

I nodded. Someday I would have to get to know her better so I could have a long conversation with her over coffee and donuts. I'm not making fun. I really loved her deep, mid-western accent. And now of course, there was the added curiosity to find out if she and her husband had dipped their toes into the marital trading pool. "You must be making some improvements," I said. "We heard you working away last night."

That bright smile dropped from her face so fast and hard I thought she might have had a stroke. "Heard what, Barb?

I hesitated. "A chain saw...we thought." Was Howard wrong? Was it a leaf blower? It was probably a leaf blower. I'm always right.

She shook her head, but not very convincingly. "Oh, no, I don't think so. Not in our backyard. Nope. Musta been someone else."

Hmm. I didn't say I heard the saw in her yard.

"Maybe," I agreed. "Could have been the Perkins."

"Oh, ya know, it mightve been them now thatcha mention it." She seemed relieved, but she was ending our conversation and skedaddling anyway. She snatched her mail from the box and pasted on the blinding smile. "Bye, Barb! Good seein' ya!"

Howard was limping down the driveway as she dashed off. I stared after her, wondering what the heck was up.

"How is..." Howard was trying to be interested, but he had the worst time remembering our neighbor's names. "What's her name?"

I lifted the mailbox door back up and clamped it closed. "Melody. Penobscott."

"Did you ask for any deck repairing tips?"

"I mentioned that we heard a saw and she said it wasn't them. But she seemed a little weird about it."

He took the mail from my hand and leafed through the contents. "They sure burn the candles at both ends, I'll tell you. She was up before dawn loading something into the trunk of her car."

Now I was the one to be surprised. "You were up before dawn?"

"Woke up around four. Couldn't get back to sleep. When I went to get a glass of water, I looked out the window because I heard something in their driveway."

Melody's odd reaction to the saw inquiry took a backseat to my concern that Howard wasn't sleeping well. Insomnia had been a problem right after he came home from the hospital, but I thought he'd been sleeping better in the last month.

"Maybe they killed that guy whose parts you found in the woods— they're sawing him up slowly and spreading limbs throughout Rustic Woods for the foxes to eat."

I slapped him playfully on the arm. "Stop that. That's not funny!"

He stopped smiling and grew more serious. "No, and neither is this—Clarence left a message on our machine. Colt was supposed to meet him yesterday for lunch followed by an interview with a reporter at the TV station for a piece they're doing on local PIs, but he never showed."

Clarence Heatherington was Colt's long lost son born out of wedlock. Sounds like a cliché plot trick, I know, but it's all true. Clarence was also the new movie reviewer for Channel 3 serving the Washington, DC Metro area. Admittedly, Colt was way more than surprised—actually, horrified is a better word—that he had fathered a son he never knew, but he chilled pretty quickly. Despite the fact that they are as different as baby pandas and werewolves, Clarence grew on him, as did the idea of being a father. Fairly soon, Colt was taking a Bill Huxtable approach to fatherhood and it didn't matter a hoot that his kid was twenty-eight years old. Clarence even lived with him for over a month while he hunted for an apartment closer to his job at Channel 3. And as for that interview, Colt also loved to talk about himself, so the fact that he'd miss lunch with Clarence and a chance to wax enthusiastic on all things Colt Baron, was a bigger red flag than his forgetting to make us tacos.

This news was seriously unsettling. "I wonder why Clarence didn't try my cell phone? He has my number." I pulled the cell from my purse and realized I had set it for silent mode while waiting in the doctor's office. Sure enough, two missed calls from Clarence. I didn't listen to those though, because I spotted something that relaxed my knitted brow: a text from Colt.

I opened the message.

Time to start worrying again.

The message read, *sos.*

CHAPTER FIVE

"SOS?" I blurted.

Howard peered over my shoulder. "What are you doing?"

"It's a text from Colt!" I could hear the distress in my own voice as it cracked.

"What does it say?"

"SOS! Didn't you hear me?" I stomped a foot and began mumbling all sorts of half-thoughts and incoherencies. "S-O-" I started. "What does that-"

I attempted a reply to the message, but must have touched the wrong button and I was sent back to my main screen. "Stupid phone! I can't-" I clicked to view messages again, but my screen went dark. "SOS. Something's...what is wrong with this phone?!" I shook the phone like it was a catatonic person that needed a jolt. Admittedly, I was out of control.

Howard relieved me of the wayward device and clicked calmly, stopping to read the message, then clicking again.

"What are you doing?" I asked.

"Texting him back."

"SOS. What does that mean? He's in trouble, right?"

"Maybe, maybe not." Howard perused through the menu and tapped another button, then placed the phone to his ear.

"Are you calling the police?"

He shook his head. "Trying his cell phone. If he texted, he must have it on now." A moment later, he shook his head again, then talked into the phone. "It's Howard. We got your text. Call Barb's phone." He hung up and handed it back to me. "Don't panic. He could have lost his cell. Someone found it and now they're having some fun."

For a minute, Howard's scenario proposal calmed me. Of course. Silly kids playing games. But then my mind shifted back to the scarier alternative. "He might not have lost it, though. And this could be real."

He nodded, his face firm and serious, his eyes fixed on mine. "In which case, what we don't do is lose our cool. I left a message for Lamon. As soon as he calls me, I'll ask him to run that license plate." He held up a key chain with a single key dangling. Colt's spare condo key. "Meanwhile, let's go back over and see if there's anything lying around his place that could give us a clue."

Thank goodness Howard had found us something to do. Sitting around and waiting for Eric to call didn't exactly make me feel empowered.

Callie drove up just then in the Camry. I had forgotten that she was putting in some volunteer hours at the local library, which reminded me that I needed to get in the house and check on Bethany and Amber just to make sure they'd eaten and didn't need anything. When Callie climbed out of the car, she walked with us up to the door. "So this is weird," she began. "I dropped Isabella off at her house and Colt's car was parked in the street out front."

Howard and I eyed each other. "Are you sure it was his?" asked Howard.

"Dad," she sighed in her teen-aged grown-ups-are-so-silly voice. "How many 1969 red GTOs are running around Rustic Woods with a 'Here comes da Judge' bumper sticker? When I asked her mom if they knew Colt, she said no, but the car has been parked there since yesterday afternoon."

Howard stopped at the door. "Is it right in front of their house, or a neighbor's house?"

"Their house," she said.

"What are you thinking?" I asked.

"If the car was parked in front of a neighbor's house, he might be visiting someone else. That still may be the case."

Luckily, Callie had stepped into the house, so I didn't have to whisper the next question. "You're thinking he had a date and stayed the night?"

Howard shrugged. He was diving into his quiet, unresponsive thinking mode. I might not hear from him for a while. We went into the house just long enough for me to check on all three girls and leave instructions for Callie to be in charge. We were going out.

"To check out Colt's car?" she asked.

"Maybe."

"Is something wrong?"

"Probably not," I answered as believably as I could.

She called out to me as I was walking toward the door. "Mom?"

"Yeah?"

"Don't get shot at again, okay?"

Ah. How sweet. She does care.

Callie and Isabella Fetty had been friends since the first grade so I knew exactly where she lived and it only took us a few minutes to get there. Just as Callie had said, Colt's car was positioned at the curb right in front of the Fetty's house on Sassafras Lane. Both doors were locked. Peeking inside the windows, we saw some papers strewn on the floor of the passenger's side, what looked to be an empty soda cup on the passenger's seat, and a camera and pen in the backseat.

"Do you know Isabella's mom?" Howard asked.

I frowned a little. "Yes, and so do you. She's been to our house so many times I can't count."

"What's her name?"

"Christina."

"Is she the tall one with short blond hair and glasses?"

"No, Sherlock. She's short with long brown hair, no glasses." I sighed. "How did they let you into the FBI anyway? On your good looks? Because it sure wasn't for your observation skills." I patted him on the back to let him know I still loved him even though he probably couldn't pick The Queen of England out of a lineup. "Christina's nice, but she bobs her head a lot when she talks."

"Got it. Let's go talk to her."

I knocked on the door and immediately heard the deep bellowing of two large dogs. I'd forgotten about their Great Danes, Frank and Stein. Should have warned Howard.

The door opened and Christina smiled at us both.

Too late.

"Barb!" (head bob) "Howard!" (bob, bob) "What brings you by? Did Callie forget something?" She dropped her smile for a moment while she reprimanded one of the horse-dogs. "Sit, Frank, sit!" Frank didn't sit, but her smile reappeared anyway when she turned her attention back to us. She stepped back and opened the door wider. "Come in, come in." (bob, bob, bob)

Howard motioned for me to go first. I wasn't sure whether that was a show of gallant manners or a healthy respect for the beasts inside. I knew that Frank and Stein were both sweet dogs, so Howard didn't need to fear an attack. On the other hand, they had very inquisitive noses.

Once we were standing in the foyer of their split-level home, I proceeded with our inquiry while the canines proceeded with a little investigation of their own.

"We're not here for Callie," I began. "She noticed that our friend's car was parked out front, and we've actually been a little worried about him."

Christina's head bobbed throughout my explanation while Frank nosed Howard's crotch. Howard tried to push the animal's nose away with his free hand, but Frank's radar was locked on target.

"Yup, yup," said Christina bobbing. "Uh huh, uh huh. The car has been there since yesterday." (bob, bob) "Uh, huh, yup. Yesterday." She glanced down at Frank as if just realizing that he was probing Howard's gonads. "Frank! No!" She yanked on his collar, but Christina was small and Frank was the polar opposite of small. Frank did not move. Meanwhile, Stein had been circling Howard like a vulture, seemingly to choose his sniff with more calculation. Christina tugged harder on

Frank's collar, yelling, "Sit!" This time he fell back on his haunches as ordered.

"I'm sorry," she apologized to Howard. "They're really sweet dogs, they're just so darned big! So why are you worried about your friend?"

At that very moment, Stein determined that Howard's rear end was where he should land his cavernous nostrils. And he did. I think Howard actually squealed. Frank, probably not wanting to miss out on the fun, left his sit-position and shot straight for Howard's crotch again.

I'd been the turkey in a Frank and Stein sandwich before, so I did feel sorry for Howard, but I wanted to get my information on Colt. I pressed forward, leaving my husband to fend for himself. "He's been missing for almost twenty-four hours now," I explained, "and his son is concerned because he missed an important meeting today. It's just not like him—his name is Colt. Did you happen to see him?"

Her head bobbed once, twice, three times. "Uh huh, uh huh. Yup, yup."

"You did?" I asked with hope.

"Oh! No! No." Now she was shaking her head vigorously. "No. I was just listening to your story. I never saw who parked the car there, I'm sorry." Her eyes suddenly blazed in horror. "Oh, Howard! Lordy, I'm so sorry! Frank and Stein seem to really like you a whole lot, don't they?"

Poor Howard was attempting, without much success, to put his buttocks out of sniffing range by shoving back against the corner between the wall and front door. He could have done some damage with his cane if he'd tried, but to his credit, he resisted temptation.

"Isabella!" shouted Christina up the stairs. "Would you come get your dogs off Mr. Marr?"

Isabella was down in a flash and with some struggle, pulled them to the back of the house and out the sliding glass door to the fenced back yard.

Thankful, Howard brushed himself off and asked a line of questions I never would have thought of. "Do you know most of your neighbors?"

"Yup. Uh, uh. Yup, yup. All of them, yup. Why?"

"Are any of them single women, not married?"

"Oh! Nope, nope. Not here. Families all around. Or married couples with grown kids. Uh huh, uh huh."

"Thank you," he said with a very officious tip of the head. I think he was quietly savoring the moment. "We appreciate your help. If you do see anyone getting in or leaving in the car, would you call us?"

"Sure, Uh huh, uh huh. Sure!"

We made a quick getaway from the Fetty house, but she waved as we headed back to our own car. "I hope your friend is okay!"

"Maybe Colt broke into their house and the dogs ate him," Howard grumbled.

"They're not vicious," I laughed. "Just curious."

We hadn't learned much except that Colt was unlikely to have spent the night at one of the other houses on Sassafras Lane. In my mind, this was more reason to accept the fact that his text was a call for help. When I expressed this worry to Howard, he didn't disagree. Next stop was Colt's condo. We had decided to hold off calling Clarence until we had better information—so far we didn't have much except the location of the car and the alarming text.

On the drive over, Howard tried Colt's cell phone again to no avail. Still straight to voicemail.

Inside, the condo was on the cool side. I looked at the thermostat—off. Howard threw the untouched newspaper we'd found on the doormat onto a small table next to the front door. "I'll check bedroom and bathroom," he said. "You look around out here."

I sniffed around the tiny kitchen. A bowl with some dried chunks of cereal around the sides rested in the sink. By the looks of it, I was guessing it had been there since the morning before. The counters were clean, the coffee pot had a smidgen of coffee left in the carafe, and a cutting board lay to one side with a knife and one dehydrated piece of apple on top. The refrigerator was what I expected for a single man: nearly empty. A carton of milk less than half full, three Coronas, a chunk of cheddar cheese, and an orange. No taco fixings except for the cheese, but that didn't really mean anything. He'd probably planned on stopping at the store for those items on his way to our house. The freezer was filled to the brim with frozen pizzas and microwaveable dinners. Now I knew how he ate when he wasn't at our place whipping up yummy meals.

Howard came out of the bathroom. "Find anything?" I asked.

"Not out of the ordinary. The sink and his toothbrush are bone dry, though. That tells me he hasn't been here since yesterday."

I closed the freezer door as Howard scooted around me. He headed into the living area, which contained a sofa, a TV, and a desk with a hutch. Howard went straight to the closed laptop on the desk. He picked up a business card that had been placed on top. I followed him into the living area and looked over his shoulder at the card. It featured a logo with red, sexy kissing lips. Swirling underneath then upward in a black cursive font were the words, *Saturday Night Fever.* Howard flipped the card over to reveal an address scrawled in blue ink: 233 Dusty Pines Place. I knew that road. It was in Rustic Woods not far from Lake Muir. Under the address was scribbled what must have been a date and a time: Nov 6 9:30 p.

"November 6th," I said. "That's today's date. Do you think the p mean's pm?"

Howard nodded and looked around the room. Then he smiled and looked right at me and grinned. "Uh huh, uh huh. Yup, yup," he said, bobbing his head up and down.

My husband made a funny. He had a sense of humor after all. I chuckled. "What do you think Saturday Night Fever is?"

"Saw that name on a discussion board last night. It's a club for swingers."

"In Rustic Woods?"

He nodded again.

"Get out! Seriously?" I let the oddity of that idea sink in for a minute then voiced some hypotheses. "So either Colt is delving into some...

interesting hobbies...or maybe this club has something to do with the job he's working on."

Howard's eyebrows lifted slightly in response as he slipped the card into his back jeans pocket and then opened the laptop. When he worked, my husband was some kind of sexy, I have to say. His reserved but serious attention to detail was turning me on. If I hadn't been so concerned for Colt, I would have suggested a quickie in the bedroom. Or the living room. Or the kitchen...

I fanned myself to cool down and took to rifling through some envelopes and papers in the hutch but it all looked like bills and invoices to clients. In a small nook of the hutch was a bowl. I reached in and pulled out a key which I showed to Howard. "That looks like the key to his car, don't you think?"

He agreed while tapping a finger waiting for the laptop to power up. A few minutes of inspection gave us nothing much to go on and Howard was concerned about Colt's privacy, if in fact, he was just gone for a few days or working on a particularly sticky job, so we didn't try to access email or documents. Basically, we'd found nothing that told us where Colt had gone or what he was up to.

My cell phone vibrated in my purse. When I pulled it out, the caller ID showed Clarence's number. I answered. "Hi Clarence." I tried to sound chipper, but I don't think it worked.

"Did you get my messages?" His voice, although sort of shaky anyway, was even shakier than usual.

"Yes, I did. We're at-"

He cut me off. "I got a text. I don't like it. Guy says it's bad."

"Guy is there?" I asked, not really that surprised.

Guy Mertz was the true crime reporter for Channel 10, and the two of them had met when we all found ourselves trying to solve the murder of a boozy movie director. Despite the fact that they now worked for rival television stations, they'd remained quite good friends, which fits since they're both, well...quirky.

"Yeah. I asked him to come over 'cuz something just isn't right here and he's the crime dude, you know."

I said to Howard, "Clarence got a text from Colt," then talked back into the phone. "What does the text say?"

"I think it's a distress signal," he said. "Guy says it's a distress signal. What do we do?"

I could hear Guy in the background telling him to tell me what the text said.

"Do what Guy says, Clarence. Tell me what was in the text."

"Maybe you should write it down. Do you have a pen?"

"Tell me what the text says, Clarence!"

He recited a set of letters. "S-O-S-N-D."

CHAPTER SIX

Clarence was too upset to continue a calm and rational conversation, so I had him put Guy on the phone. Guy informed me that they had attempted several texts back to Colt's number without response and that their many calls to his cell phone went directly to voicemail without ringing.

"We're going to try his home phone next," Guy said.

"You'll only get Howard or me on the phone if you do that."

"You're at his place?"

"Yup. And he is not. It looks like he hasn't been here since yesterday morning."

"That's not a good sign."

"He's a single guy. On the surface we're not sure it's bad, but we found his car parked on Sassafras Lane—it's a neighborhood that he wouldn't be likely to hang out in. And it's been there since yesterday afternoon. Too many things here aren't right. We found a key to his car here, so we're heading back over there now to see if we can find anything important."

"Anything we can do?"

"You can keep Clarence from having a coronary. He's too young to die."

Howard pulled the card from his back pocket and waved it in front of my face. "Oh!" I said, understanding his sign language. "Find out anything you can on a swinger's club in Rustic Woods called Saturday Night Fever. And let us know right away if you hear from Colt again."

I could hear him repeating the words, probably while he scribbled on something, "Saturday Night Fever. Like the movie, right?"

"Right."

"Did I hear that right? You said a swinger's club?"

"Your ears are working."

"And why, exactly?"

The phone vibrated in my hand, indicating another call coming in. I peeked quickly at the display and saw the caller was my mother. "I need to take this call, Guy. I'll explain later, just check it out. Talk to you soon."

"Over and out."

I clicked to my mother's call. "What's up mom?"

"Is that the way you answer a phone?"

"I'm forty-six years old, mother. Do my phone manners still require your reproach?"

"Even a forty-six year old woman can learn and change."

"Mom, I'm kind of busy right now. Why are you calling, please?" My jaw was tight with irritation.

"I'm with Alka at the hospital. She had some sort of episode during our art class."

"You couldn't have opened with that? What kind of episode?"

"Heart. But she's in good hands here with a cardiologist on call."

I was so mad at my mother for preceding the 'Mama Marr had a heart attack message' with a rebuke of my phone manners that I did what any mature, sensible, grown woman would do: I hung up on her.

"We have to go, your mother's in the hospital."

His face went dark. "Which hospital?"

Darn! That would have been a good thing to ask. Reluctantly, I called my mother back.

"What's up, Barbara?" she answered.

Oh, I was going to get her good one day.

I gritted my teeth. "Which hospital, mom?"

"Fairfax General. We're still in the ER."

Howard called the girls while I ignored all posted speed limits between Rustic Woods and Fairfax General Hospital. What ordinarily was a twenty-five minute drive took us only fifteen. Luckily we weren't pulled over by a policeman for speeding. If we had been, I would have told him that if he wanted to prevent a true crime, he should follow us to the hospital and intervene before I killed my mother.

Once in the Emergency Room, we were directed to a curtained-off treatment area where we found Mama Marr lying on a partially raised gurney bed, electrodes pasted here and there, wires running to machines that beeped and booped. She and my mother, who sat in a chair next to the bed, were enjoying a mutual giggle.

"Diane," said Mama Marr, "you know how to make me laugh like a leetle girl." Her eyes lit up when she saw us and she clapped her hands together merrily. "Sammy! You are here! Barbara! Come, come!"

By 'Sammy', of course, Mama Marr meant 'Howard'. See, Howard grew up with the name Sammy Donato. His father, Mario Donato, was whacked by the infamous Tito Buttaro. Set on revenge and aided by his mother who supported her only son fully, he changed his name to Howard Marr and joined the FBI to hunt Tito down legally. Don't believe it? Trust me, I had a hard time swallowing the truth too, especially since I discovered all of this after being kidnapped by Tito's angry, chain-smoking wife and her two goons. Those two goons turned out to be really nice guys and one of them is now my friend, Frankie Romano, who I would trust my life with any day of the week.

Bottom line, Mama Marr wasn't experiencing dementia, she just slips a lot and calls Howard by the name she gave him when he was born. I'm actually glad he changed his name, because I can't really imagine being Barbara Donato, wife of Sammy Donato, Mafia Hunter. Somehow I'd feel destined for a reality show or at the very least, a gig on Jerry Springer.

Howard handed me his cane and moved to his mother's side without a hint of a limp. He kissed her on the forehead. "How are you feeling, Ma?"

"Peaches, peaches!" she said, which, translated, meant "peachy". "The doctor say I'm healthy as a horsey." See what I mean about the healthy horse rumors? "Maybe you should just get on my back and ride me out of thees place!"

Yikes, I didn't like the image that remark evoked. A little too Oedipal.

Howard was unfazed and fully focused on getting some answers. "I'm going to find your doctor. I'll be back in a minute."

His dedication to his mother was heartening, but I couldn't help but reminisce of the birth of our first child when a less attentive Howard spent two hours positioning the chair in the labor and delivery room so it would face the TV at just the right viewing angle. Fine, I'm probably exaggerating. It was probably more like forty-five minutes of chair positioning time. The next two hours were spent, with his back to me, cheering on the Redskins while I lay there, contracting painfully every six minutes and not dilating an iota. Where was his concern then, when I needed ice chips and foot rubs? But no, I'm not bitter.

"Mama," I asked during Howard's exit, "what happened?"

"Barbara! Thees is so funny! Your mama and me," she pointed to my mother whose presence I purposely ignored, "were getting our pencils and pads of paper ready in the art classroom for the drawing of the figure." She giggled so hard she had to stop talking. Once she regained her composure, she continued, but still very giggly. "Thees figure, is a man, and well, he dropped off his robe and right there this close to my face..." she placed nearly kissing index finger and thumb out for me to indicate the very minor distance, "...was his *prącia!*"

"That's his penis, dear," my mother explained.

I cringed and my body tightened, the whole boy-in-the-doctor's-office trauma flashing before my eyes. I continued to ignore her.

"You're right, Mama," I said soothingly, "that is a funny story, but what about your heart?"

"Well, I had this pain, right here," she indicated her chest, "shooting in me. You know, when I was looking at the *prącia.*"

"The penis," said my mother, the educator.

The time for ignoring had ended. I spun around so fast that if my head hadn't been attached it would have flown off and landed in China. "I know what a *prącia* is, Mom!" I yelled.

"It's true, Diane," said Mama more seriously now. "She knows the *prącia.* She found one in the woods yesterday."

Thankfully for my mother's safety, Howard returned with the cardiologist who explained that Mama Marr had not experienced a coronary episode, but a gastric one, most likely brought on by a combination of the beans and spicy chilies in her burrito bowl from Olé Olé, a popular Tex Mex restaurant on the outskirts of Rustic Woods.

I was incredulous. "You ate Mexican food?"

"Your mama said I should be more for the adventure and I agree. It was very good, this burrito bowl. So, what's a little gas, no?"

Content that his mother was, in fact, as healthy as a horse, Howard asked if she would excuse him, me, and my mom for a couple of minutes. We convened outside near the nurses desk. "Diane, can you take my mom back home and keep an eye on her for an hour or two? Barb and I have something we need to do." I assumed he meant rummaging through Colt's car, since that had been next on our agenda prior to the Mama Marr Tex Mex acid reflux fiasco.

"Absolutely!" she gushed, as if she wasn't at all responsible for the hospital visit to begin with. She patted his hand. "I'll take good care of her."

I was beginning to wonder if that was true.

Just then a nurse appeared out of nowhere. "Diane!" A warm, broad smile tore across the nurse's face and she swooped in for a hug. "It's so good to see you!"

My mom hugged her back. "You too, Martha. I'll be seeing you next Tuesday. Tell Wendy I said, 'Hi.'"

"Will do," answered the nurse. She stood, looking expectantly for an introduction.

My mother picked up the hint. "Martha, this is my daughter Barbara and her husband Howard. This is Martha, one of the nurses in the pediatric NICU."

The look on my face must have registered my misunderstanding of the word. "Neo-natal intensive care unit," explained Martha the very nice nurse. "Your mother volunteers several times a week. She's an angel. You're so lucky to have her for a mother."

I wondered how much my mother paid her to say that. It spilled out too easily, like an amateur bit of dialogue in a movie on Lifetime.

"What do you do in a pediatric intensive care?" I asked my mom, trying to bite back my skepticism that she did anything more than sort their mail.

She brushed me off. "Nothing much."

"Nothing much?" scoffed Martha the overly enthusiastic nice nurse. "She spends hours with the babies who don't have mommies to hold them."

I couldn't believe there were that many babies who didn't have mommies to hold them, but Martha corrected me. While there was the occasional baby who was born underweight or malnourished to mothers who did not want their children, there was also a growing number of babies born to mothers who were addicted to opiates. Their mothers had lost parental rights and the poor babies had to spend weeks in the NICU while being weaned off of the drugs.

"There aren't enough nurses to go around sometimes to hold the babies as much as they need, so your mother and some other wonderful ladies," she stopped herself for a second, "and gentlemen too" she added, "offer their time and love."

"You mean Crack babies?"

Martha winced and shook her head. "Some people call them 'Oxycontin babies' but I don't like the term. Here at Fairfax General, we call them 'babies-in-need.'"

I expected my mother to tell me that I should try volunteering sometime, as I could obviously use the exposure to human kindness. But she didn't.

During our brief talk with Martha, not less than four nurses, a doctor, and a janitor (who looked suspiciously like that guy on the TV show *Scrubs*) waved to my mother and shouted a friendly, "Hello, Diane!"

On our drive from Fairfax back to Rustic Woods, I tried to focus on Colt's mysterious disappearance, but my mind kept drifting to visions of Diane Pettingford—hard-line, no-nonsense mother—gently holding and cradling poor little drug-addicted babies. The two images just didn't mesh.

Maybe, I thought, it was time to get to know my own mother a little bit better.

Then I thought, *Barb, are you out of your freaking mind?*

CHAPTER SEVEN

Colt's old, worn key stuck in the GTO's door lock. I feared for a minute while Howard jiggled it back and forth, that we would have to resort to the coat hanger method of breaking in. His persistence prevailed, however, and soon we were not-so-systematically digging through the belongings in Colt's precious automobile. The papers on the passenger's side floor amounted to nothing more than a three-month-old receipt for an oil change and tire rotation at Speedy Lube, two empty McDonald's bags, a paper ripped from a steno pad with an address scribbled on it, and a faded flier advertising the Rustic Woods Summer Jamboree at Rustic Woods Town Center which had probably been placed on his windshield while parked in the Town Center lot months earlier.

Howard used his cell phone to search the address on the steno paper and came up with the office of NOVA Urology, Drs. Robert Markleson, MD and Kyung Kong, MD, F.A.C.S.

"Kyung Kong?" I asked with a half-chuckle. "Seriously?"

"It's what it says."

"Poor guy. I hope he uses a nickname like Joe or Willy or something." I thought about that and realized that Willy Kong was probably no better. "What does F.A.C.S. stand for?"

Howard googled the acronym zippy quick on his smart phone and had an answer before I could vocalize my next thought which was, *Is Colt seeing a urologist?*

"Surgeon. Kong is a licensed surgeon."

"Ouch."

"Tell me about it," Howard cringed.

"Do you think Colt is seeing one of these guys as a patient?"

"Either that, or working for him, or following him." He pointed to my purse. "Get your phone out, we'll eliminate or confirm the first possibility."

Whoa, my husband was so cool and in charge. I liked this. Much better than the depressed, mopey complainer of the last couple of months. He instructed me to dial the number of the medical practice and ask for insurance and billing. Privacy laws wouldn't allow practitioners to disclose their patients' names, so I was to be sneaky about how I asked for my information. Roger that. I had my instructions and proceeded with caution. The phone rang five times before someone picked up.

"Nnmmm dmmnnsh mmmmmm nn mmmrnong, how may I direct your call?" mumbled the woman who answered. Wonderful, I thought, yet another bored receptionist incapable of coherency. As a mother who must routinely deal with doctor offices, you would think I'd get used to not understanding the people on the other end of the phone, but I don't. It always annoys me greatly.

Assuming I had successfully reached NOVA Urology, Drs. Markleson and Kong, I continued forth on my quest. "Insurance and billing, please," I said ever so politely.

An immediate CLICK was followed by music in my ears for five minutes, interrupted every so often with a gentle, courteous, and intelligible, "Thank you for calling NOVA Urology. We want you to know that we value your time. Please remain on the line, and someone will be with you shortly. Thank you for waiting." Blah, blah, blah. After four minutes on hold, I severely doubted that anyone valued my time. The recording lady was pleasant though—they should have hired her to answer the phones.

Finally, a woman who sounded suspiciously like the first receptionist came on the line. "Carla," she announced sharply. "How may I assist you?" At least those were the words she uttered, but the tone implied: "You're bothering me during my Facebook time, whatdaya want?"

I pressed forward with the sweetness of sugar off the cane. "This is Mrs. Baron. My husband Colt Baron was in for an appointment and I have the insurance company on the phone right now looking at the claim." Howard had guided me on exactly what to say, but I feel my interpretation and delivery were Oscar-worthy, thank you very much. "They say he was in on October sixteenth but I think that date is incorrect. Could you just check for me?"

"Spell the last name."

"B-A-R-O-N. First name Coltrane."

I could hear the clicking of fingers on a keyboard. "That date is incorrect. He saw Dr. Markleson on November third and that claim hasn't even been submitted by our office yet. Your insurance company must be looking at a claim from a different doctor. Is that all?"

"That's all. Thank you for your-"

CLICK.

That answered that question. Colt had seen a urologist. A urologist with some very curt employees, by the way. Now I was really worried, and not about the rude employees. My only experience with urologists was when my favorite Uncle Mort had prostate cancer. He complained quite loudly and far too descriptively about the examinations that led to the diagnosis. I loved the man, but I knew *way* more about his doctor's visits than I wanted to.

"Does a man see a urologist for routine well-checks?" I asked, exposing my motherliness. Only a mother and her pediatrician talk about "well-checks."

"No," said Howard, his face somber. He picked up the digital camera with the long lens and started skimming through the most recent photos taken.

Beginning at 10:17 the morning before, a series of pictures were shot of an Asian man dressed in a gray suit.

I ventured a speculation. "Kyung Kong?"

Howard kept scrolling. "It's a guess. Certainly we seem to be getting warmer. At the very least, I'm guessing this man has something to do with the woman we saw at the condo."

Three of the first pictures showed the man sitting on a bench alone. In the fourth picture, he was looking at his watch. I knew instantly where those photos had been taken; the statue behind the man was a dead give-away. He was sitting on one of the many benches that circled the edge of Lake Muir on the North side of Rustic Woods. The statue had been built to honor naturalist John Muir. By my estimate of the angle the photo was taken from, Colt had probably been parked on West Shore Drive, a decent distance away. He had a good telephoto lens for sure.

The next picture was taken at 10:22 and a woman had entered the frame. She was blond and dressed in black sweat pants and a t-shirt, which was odd considering how chilly it would have been at 10:22 that morning. From the picture, her age was hard to pinpoint, although I was guessing over thirty. The hair color appeared to be concocted from a bottle. A large, flowery tote-bag was slung over her left shoulder. In the next picture they were both standing and in the next, both sitting. The woman hugged herself, probably to keep warm. There were three more pictures of them sitting, then one of her reaching into her bag, and another of her handing him a large manila envelope.

Five pictures, all taken at 10:25, were of the woman rising then leaving. In one of them she had turned back around and pointed to the Asian man as if she was scolding him. Another picture showed her climbing into a red sports sedan. The license plate wasn't visible from the angle of the photograph.

After that, Colt had apparently begun following the woman because the next picture, shot at 10:35, showed her walking into a Sunny Way grocery store. Another picture at three minutes after eleven showed her coming out of a Quickie Mart carrying a heavily loaded plastic grocery bag. The last picture, taken at eleven fifty-nine in the morning, showed the woman coming out of yet another grocery mart with a similar bag. And that ended our photo journal of Colt's whereabouts on Friday. What happened to him after 11:59?

"What kind of car do you think that is?" I asked Howard.

"Mercedes E-Class. E550. Two thousand eleven."

I looked at him, completely taken by surprise, but understanding that there was a reason he knew this fact.

"I'll never know why it is that you knew that off the top of your head, will I?"

"Nope."

Those were the only pictures taken with Colt's camera the day before, so our last photo-record of his whereabouts ended at 11:59 on Friday, November 5th.

This entire time, we'd been standing outside of Colt's car which was parked on Sassafras Lane in front of the Fetty's house. I felt a little self-conscious, but no one in the few cars that drove by really seemed to give us a second glance. We considered having Howard drive the car back to our house, but changed our minds. Instead, Howard left a note, wedged into the steering wheel instructing Colt to call us ASAP if he returned.

We locked up the GTO and were ready to leave in my van when the door to the Fetty's house opened and Christina ran out with a smile on her face, waving to us. "Barb! Howard!" She was panting by the time she reached us at the sidewalk. "You missed him, some hooligan-looking man checking out your friend's car very suspiciously." She lowered her voice to a near whisper when she said "suspiciously" and bobbed her head three times.

"How long ago?" asked Howard.

"Hour ago, maybe? Uh huh, uh huh. Yup. Hour ago."

"What did he look like? Height? Weight? Skin color? Anything you can tell me."

She scrunched up her face and looked very uncomfortable as if he were asking her to recite a monologue from Macbeth or King Lear. Then all sorts of strange sounds came out of her mouth. "Er, eh, yeuuh, er...gee, yeah, ieeee..." Her face contorted this way and that in what I assumed was her way of summoning a decent description. I thought she might just give up the ghost and say, "Hell if I know!" when she caught sight of something far down the sidewalk. "Him!" she pointed. "That's him down there, uh huh, uh huh."

Howard and I both turned our heads in the direction she indicated. A young man—or perhaps even a teenager—took off running at the far end of the sidewalk.

Howard had been managing just fine without his cane ever since the hospital, but I couldn't picture him sprinting fast enough to bring this fugitive down. I dashed like I'd never dashed before, and all I can say is, it was a good thing I'd been walking more those last few days, because my legs weren't generally used to such spontaneous workouts. Even so, he was still faster than me, so I had to rely on my wits and my lungs.

My wits, because I suddenly realized that I recognized this kid. My lungs because, well...

"Hey! Wait! Stop!" I bellowed. "Please! I think you know my daughter, Callie Marr! I just want to ask you...(I was panting heavily now)...a quick...question!"

Wits and lungs won that battle and the kid halted his gallop, allowing me to catch up. "Mrs. Marr?" he asked as I slowly closed the gap between us, gasping for air.

"Yeah. Callie's mom," I panted. "You go to school with her, right?"

He nodded. "Kyle."

That was it. Kyle. They'd been science fair partners her Freshman year and she'd been mortified because all he ever talked about was cars, cars, cars. I was beginning to see where this trail would lead, but I followed it anyway.

"Kyle. Right. How are you?"

His answer was hesitant and I can't say I blamed him. A crazy woman had just chased him down, for crying out loud. "Fine..." he said.

Howard finally reached us and I introduced the two. "Kyle, Callie's dad. Callie's dad, Kyle."

Still appearing alarmed by the chase, Kyle ventured out on a limb. "Is this because I was looking at the GTO?"

"Kind of," I said. "We're concerned about our friend who owns it. We haven't seen him since yesterday."

He perked up a bit. "Old guy, blond hair?"

"Depends on what you mean by old," I said.

"You know, your age, probably," answered Kyle, stone-faced serious. I heard Howard suppress a laugh.

"You saw him?"

Kyle nodded. "Yesterday after school. Must have been about two-thirty? Something like that."

"Did you see where he went?" Howard pressed.

"Not exactly. I'm taking care of some pets down at the end of the street." He pointed past the Fetty's house. "I saw him get out of the car and said, 'Nice wheels, man' and he said, 'Thanks, man,' and then he came this way and I kept going that way." His arms flailed around indicating who was moving where.

"You never saw him go into any of these houses around here?"

"Nah. Didn't see. But man, this car is the best, isn't it? You don't see classic GTOs like this every day. I can't help but stop and look every time I pass it, ya know? I wasn't going to steal it or anything. Was that lady saying I was trying to steal it?" He tipped his head toward Christina Fetty, who still stood on the sidewalk in front of her house watching us from afar.

"No." I tried not to laugh. "She just thought you might have some information for us."

"Cool. Well, can I go now, then? I think I forgot to lock the back door after I let the dog out earlier. My mom will kill me if I don't do this job right."

"Yeah," I said. "Thanks."

"Sure, Mrs. Marr." He strode off back in the direction he'd originally started.

"We make a pretty good team," Howard said with a smile as Kyle ambled away. "You know everyone, and I don't."

I was about to reply with an equally quippy and fun retort when a red car sped by on the cross street. The license plate was easy to read as it passed since it was personalized: FEEVRR.

But that wasn't the most interesting part of this newest development.

"Howard, was that a..."

He gave a nod and finished my sentence. "Red Mercedes E550."

Chapter Eight

The car disappeared around a bend in the road. We got to my van as quickly as we could, giving a quick "thanks" and "goodbye" to Christina, then sped off in the same direction the Mercedes had traveled. But several minutes of searching up and down the road and side streets were wasted. The car was gone.

The fact that we'd seen the same make and color of Mercedes as the one in Colt's pictures indicated to Howard that Colt might have continued his investigative work and parked far enough away from his blond, sweatpants-wearing target so as not to be detected. Of course, this was still just a theory on the table. We had no hard evidence to go on.

Howard dialed Officer Lamon to see if he'd run the first license plate belonging to the crazy Asian lady, and to see if he could add another to his list of favors. This time he was able to get Eric on the phone and the news was good. He had a name and address for Crazy Asian Lady: Shin Lee at 233 Dusty Pines Place, Rustic Woods.

I recognized the address right away, and so did Howard. It was written on the back of the Saturday Night Fever business card. So Colt was supposed to meet her at 9:30 tonight, possibly, at her home? Certainly made sense. Had she stopped by earlier in the day to cancel or change their appointment? Who knew, but at least we were beginning to connect some dots on our hunt for Colt.

Eric told Howard he would run the FEEVRR plate and file a missing persons report on Colt. He would also gladly assist us personally when his shift ended at ten. When Howard got off the phone with Eric, he tried Colt's cell again just in case. Unfortunately, the result was no different.

The clock on my dashboard read four-thirty in the afternoon, but it felt much later, probably because it was already starting to get dark and because we'd been running around all day like those proverbial un-dead chickens. It was time for rest, a good meal and some time with the kids.

My phone rang as I motored toward home. Howard checked the display. "It's Peggy, should I answer?"

"No. Hit ignore."

"You're still mad at her?"

"I'm a woman. Holding a silent grudge is not only what I do best, it's my right and my responsibility."

"Do you even know why you're holding a grudge?"

"For standing me up."

"Maybe there's a good reason. Did you ask her?"

"I told you, I know what happened. She stood me up for Dandi Booker. I just need time to cool off, that's all. Once that happens, I'll talk to her and only punish her by making snide jibes disguised as jokes and veiled snarky comments on her Facebook posts. See, you think I'm not aware that my dark side lives, but I'm very aware, Master Yoda, very aware."

"You're lucky you have any friends at all," he muttered under his breath.

Truth be told, although I joked about my 'dark side', I was quickly realizing that it was probably not a matter for joking and that Howard was righter than wronger about me living up to my word on valuing friendships.

A minute later my phone chirped, indicating a new voicemail.

"She left a message," he said.

I pulled into our driveway. "I'll listen to it later. I'm tired and hungry right now."

Howard limped slowly to the house, leaning heavily on his cane again. I was mad at myself for not insisting he let me do more of the work. He shouldn't have been doing all of that walking and certainly no running. When I tried to help him, he brushed me off.

"I'm fine," he grumbled.

But I could tell he was in pain.

Remembering that my purse was still in the van, I turned to retrieve it. From the corner of my eye, I saw Melody Penobscott tip-toeing through the leaf-covered grass between her house and mine. She waved and called out. "Yoo hoo! Barb! Yoo hoo!"

I sucked back an annoyed sigh. Despite my affinity for the way she pronounced her vowels, the thought of talking to anyone at that moment was less than appealing. I smiled anyway, because that's what nice neighbors do.

"Hi Melody. What's up?"

Her pony tail swished like a windshield wiper. "You look tired. Are you tired?"

"Yeah. Yeah I am."

"Well, I hope you don't mind me catchin' you for just a sec. See, I wanted to tell ya that I told a little lie earlier." She winced and pinched two fingers together when she said, 'little' to illustrate.

"Um, okay..."

"And I feel just awful about it, so I just had to come clean, 'cuz that's how I like to be ya know—clean."

Get to it lady, I'm tired. I stared at her, hoping she'd just come clean anyway.

"We're cutting down a tree. Little pieces at a time. There, I said it." She was waving her hand around and that pony tail flipped this way and that. "That was the sound you heard last night. Please don't report us. I just didn't want us to start out our lives as neighbors with that lie between us."

I laughed so hard I thought I'd pee my pants. "Melody, we take trees down all of the time. You don't need to do it in the dead of night, for crying out loud."

"But the Association..."

"They'll only find out if someone reports you and no one will because everyone on this street does it. In the daylight." I patted her little panic-stricken hand. "Your secret is safe with me. Did you check with your landlords, the Walkers?"

"Sure did."

"Then I wouldn't worry. Listen, I've had a long day, I'm going to head in."

"Sure, Barb, sure. Good talkin' to ya. And thanks for understandin'."

I pondered the similarity between homeowners associations and dictatorships as I made my way to the house. And for a fleeting moment, I wondered why she was so worried if she'd talked to Roz and Peter about it. Certainly they would have said the same as me. I shrugged off the thought since there were much larger problems on my mind. And a grumble in my tummy.

The amazing aroma of Mama Marr's goulash tickled my nose the minute I stepped through the front door, and all I could think was, *thank you Mama, thank you. I don't have to cook and my taste buds will sing while I gorge myself.*

That Mama Marr arrived from the hospital revved and ready to whip up a huge meal for seven people was testament to her strong constitution. Why, the woman was actually a three-time skillet-throwing champion in her small town outside Philly. Not only could she throw a mean skillet, but she could whip up a mean meal in a skillet to boot. She was an Energizer Bunny, and no amount of sciatica or black-bean-induced gastric chest pain was going to keep her down. Especially when it came to feeding her family. I wanted to show my gratitude by bringing Pavrotti back from my mother's house in his shiny gold cage and say, "Here you go Mama, Pavrotti can stay. We'll post motion sensor activated BB guns around the perimeter of his little birdie home to keep those mean ol' puddy tats away." But let's face it, we'd all seen Sylvester and Tweety in action, and while Sylvester never actually swallowed Tweety, my Indiana Jones had something Sylvester did not: a dedicated partner in crime named Mildred Pierce. The feathered tenor didn't have a chance in our feline-infested home. So I bit back my offer and just said, "Yum! Goulash! When do we eat?"

She slapped my hand as I tried to sneak a taste with the wooden spoon. "Not ready yet, Barbara. Must simmer. An hour maybe." She craned her neck to look around me. "Where's my Howard?"

"Living room, on the couch. He's a little tired."

Her face crunched up in disapproval. "Too much running around on the legs. He needs rest! Why you make him do this work running around all day?"

"I didn't make him do anything, Mama," I said, my feelings a little hurt. Okay, a lot hurt. I lowered my voice. "I actually think he's a lot happier today than I've seen him in months. It's like he has a purpose again."

Amber popped her pretty little head into the conversation between us. "Is his purpose finding Colt? Callie said Colt is disappeared and you and Daddy are trying to find him before he dies!" Her eyes were wide.

"Callie said that?" I asked.

"Amber made up the 'before he dies' part," interjected Bethany from behind a book while she sat at the kitchen table next to my mother, who was immersed in her iPad. "Callie just said that you were looking for Colt." She looked up from the book. "Did you find him?"

Amber continued to look deeply concerned so I did what mothers don't really like to do, but we do all the time and just call it "fibbing"— I lied. "We sure did!" I smiled widely down at Amber who turned her own frown upside down and hugged me tight.

"That's because you and Daddy make a great team," she said.

Hmm, that was the second time I'd heard that remark in the same day.

My mother lifted her stare from the iPad. "Where did you find him?" she asked.

The minute my answer escaped my lips, I knew I was in trouble. "Around." Yup, that's what I said. "Around." I was tired and hungry. The combination of these two deprived states of being limits one's ability to lie believably on-the-spot. It's a fact. I'm sure they've done studies.

"Around?" she asked. "Where around?"

I laughed. "His condo around. Where else?"

Don't ask me why, but this seemed to satisfy my mother.

I snuck a glance at Bethany, whose eyes were narrowed in skepticism. I could never put anything past Bethany. As a toddler she'd questioned the whole Santa story, emphasizing the discrepancy in size between the girth of the red-suited man and the width of the chimney flue. Of course, she didn't use those precise words—she was only two—but I distinctly recall the words 'girth' and 'flue'. She was Mensabound, that one. And, as my mother never failed to point out, I wasn't nearly as intelligent at the same age.

I poured two tall glasses of water and joined Howard on the couch, where we talked in hushed tones.

"I hope we hear from Eric soon," I said. "I hate this waiting game."

Howard sipped while he silently pondered. "I've been thinking," he finally said. "That I should go over and have a talk with that Shin Lee woman tonight."

"Are you kidding me?" I shook my head in vigorous disagreement. "You're not going anywhere tonight on that leg. I'll go."

"I'm not going to let you go alone. Are *you* kidding *me?*"

"Mo-om! Bethany called from the other room. "Your phone is ringing!"

I must have left my purse on the table. I was too tired to get up. "See who it is!" I shouted, then said to Howard, "Maybe it's Guy or Clarence. I thought we might have heard from them by now."

"It's Mrs. Rubenstein!" she called back.

I blew out a sigh while I contemplated talking to Peggy. Nah. I was too tired. "Don't answer it!" I yelled. "I'll call her back in a little while." I anticipated Howard's disapproving scowl. "What? I don't want to tie up the phone in case Guy or Clarence call. Or Eric. Or Colt." I continued on our who-was-kidding-who conversation. "You can't really think it's a good idea to put any more strain on that leg today, can you?"

"It just needed some rest. It's better already." He bent his knee a few times and then his ankle to prove his point. And there's no way I'm letting you go alone."

"I'll take my mace."

"You'll take your husband. You know, the one trained to maim and even kill if necessary."

"What are you going to maim her with, your cane? I'm a woman, she's a woman, we'll have a calm, rational, womanly chat."

"Because it went just that way the last time you tried to talk to her."

I planned on fighting him further, but he stopped me short. "It's decided. We'll both go. And you can bring your mace."

"And you can bring your cane."

We clinked glasses to celebrate our compromise, but all the while, Colt's texts nagged at me. If they were from him, and not from some prankster who'd stolen or stumbled upon his phone, then something was very, very wrong. I'd traveled down roads leading to Wrongville before and they were treacherous, to say the least.

I chewed on that worry bone until dinner was served. Goulash called my name, and for at least a few minutes, I thought of nothing but how savory it was. By the way, I was pretty sure that none of those ingredients were on Dr. Sadistic's "good" list of foods for Howard or me. That diet was just going to have to wait another day.

After dinner I asked my mom if she wouldn't mind sticking around to keep an eye on things around the house while Howard and I went out. We'd like to have a date night, I said, and especially with Mama Marr's little incident, better to have another adult around the house.

"You didn't find Colt, did you?"

Darn! How did she do that?

"Date night, Mom," I lied again, although I don't know why. I knew she had me, but I was resorting to old adolescent habits. When I was a teenager, I'm not sure I ever told my mother a complete truth. And again, I don't know why, because she always knew better. She was a psychic and a Marine rolled all into one with the name "Mom" slapped across her chest. "We just want to have some time to ourselves."

She narrowed her beady eyes and peered at me over her wire-rimmed glasses. We faced off: interrogator and pathetic, menopausal woman with a secret. The tension in the room was palpable. Who would break first? I thought for sure it would be me when I felt the first bead of sweat begin to burst through the skin of my upper lip, but then, just when I was about to call "Uncle," she sighed and looked away. "Fine," she said. "I'll stay. Do you have the Science Channel? There's a fascinating documentary tonight about tree ants in the Amazon. Maybe Callie would like to watch with me."

Callie? Not unless Ryan Gosling was personally holding the tree ants in every shot. Shirtless.

"Try Bethany," I said, "that's probably a little more up her alley."

She eventually conned Mama Marr into joining her.

As Howard and I were jacketing up near the front door, my mother called from the living room. "Don't worry! I'll stay until you get home or I get a call from the hospital saying a stray bullet sideswiped you while you *weren't* out searching for Colt." Then she added, "Don't forget your mace."

I made a face, but patted my jacket pocket just to double check. Yup, mace was still there.

Shin Lee's house at 233 Dusty Pines Place was a ten minute drive across town. We had decided to arrive a few minutes earlier than the 9:30 time noted on the card. If Colt wasn't in trouble, and his plan had been to meet her at that time, we'd intercept and, although relieved, give him a piece of our mind for scaring us half to death. If Colt didn't show, we'd knock on her door and see if Shin Lee had answers that would lead us to him. I wasn't anticipating the chattiest of conversations, given her stated lack of English skills, but if she lived in Rustic Woods, the woman had to be able to speak at least some of the language. She was last seen knocking on Colt's door after all, and the only languages he spoke were English and Surfer Dude.

"Shin Lee," I wondered out loud as we turned off our White Willow Lane toward Rustic Woods Parkway. "Is that Chinese?"

"Korean," Howard answered confidently.

"I don't supposed you speak Korean, do you?"

"Enough."

"Really?"

"Worked a Korean organized crime case for over a year. Picked up a fair amount. I think we'll be able to communicate, if that's what you're wondering."

I was wondering that, and many other things about my husband's once secret job, but my phone jingled again, announcing the arrival of another text. We'd put my phone in the cup holder between us for quicker access. Howard picked it up and eyed the display.

"Colt," he said, tapping to read.

"Please tell me it says, 'Hi guys, I'm home, sorry for the confusion.'"

Howard shook his head. "Sad to say, no, but he's letting us know he's the one sending the texts."

"What do you mean?"

"This one says *Curly*. He's smart and at least he's still alive."

"How's that smart? He always calls me Curly."

"Exactly. Only he calls you Curly. He's telling us this is him and not someone else with his phone."

The phone jingled again. Another text.

"Is that Colt again?"

Howard nodded. "RMPTCHTG."

"What?"

"That's what this says. RM space PT space CHTG."

"What the heck?"

"Three strings of letters."

"More code?"

"Maybe."

Howard's phone rang this time and my hopes soared that it was Colt. "Who is it?"

"Don't know," said Howard.

He'd have known if it was Colt because his name would have showed on his caller ID the same way it does on mine. Howard answered the unknown phone number. "It's Lamon," he said to me. "Here, let me put you on speaker, Eric." A second later, Howard, Officer Eric Brad Pitt Lamon, and I were conversing while I drove. "Hi, Barb," said Eric's voice. "How are you doing?"

"I'm worried, Eric. Worried."

"Understand that. Listen, I don't have an official report yet, but a woman named Cherry Sparrow has contacted Loudoun County Police claiming that her husband, Orson Sparrow has been missing for more than twenty-four hours. They've asked her to come in for possible identification of the remains you discovered yesterday."

I hadn't really been dying for that information, since finding Colt was far more important.

"How will she identify them?" asked Howard. "Markings on the hand?"

"Not the hand. Evidently there was a large brown patch on his-"

"No, no!" I interrupted. "No! Don't need to hear it!" I shouted.

"She doesn't like the word," explained Howard. "But thanks, we got the idea."

"I'm more interested in the Mercedes, Eric," I said, moving to topic back to Colt. "Did you find anything on that license plate?"

"That's the strange thing about the Sparrows, Barb," said Lamon's voice. "Cherry Sparrow claims her husband never came home after leaving in a huff, uh..." his voice trailed off briefly. "Thursday. Thursday afternoon. When she reported him missing on Friday, she told Loudoun County police that he'd come to Rustic Woods to talk to a couple who had been renting some farm land from them. In Loudoun, I mean. Apparently he was having some disagreement with them over the land— it's unclear. That couple's name is Rick and Rita Ash."

"Okay..." I said, confused. "What's strange about that?"

"The car whose plates you asked me to run belongs to a Rita Ash who lives in Rustic Woods."

CHAPTER NINE

Eric asked where Colt's car was parked. When we told him Sassafras Lane, he went silent for a minute.

"You still there?" Howard asked.

"Yeah. Hang on." Then he gave a low whistle. "That's just one street over from where Rick and Rita Ash live."

Howard leaned back in his seat. "I had a feeling. Anything you can do?"

"I can send a car out to the house. I'll get back to you when I have more information." He clicked off.

Just minutes away from our destination, Howard and I did a verbal run-through of Colt's photo diary from that morning. He'd been following an Asian man who rendezvoused with a white woman. She'd given him an envelope. The white woman sped away in a red Mercedes and Colt followed. Was the Asian man related to Shin Lee? He could be her husband possibly. Or maybe he was Dr. Kyung Kong? Or both? Had Colt been hired by Shin Lee to follow him? He often complained that many of his clients were jealous spouses.

Continuing on, Red Mercedes Lady, who we now presumed was Rita Ash, traveled to three different grocery stores. She left each carrying a heavy bag. The last photo had been taken at 11:59 in the morning, just before noon. So what did Colt do between 11:59 and somewhere around 2:30, when Kyle saw him park in front of the Fetty's house? We'd reached 233 Dusty Pines Place, but no hard conclusions about Colt or how much danger he might be in.

To say that 233 Dusty Pines Place was a house would be grossly unfair to the dwelling. It was somewhere between a McMansion and a real mansion and *way* bigger than our own modest humble abode. Shin Lee lived in some sweet digs. A long, long, long paved drive wound from the road toward what could only be described as small parking lot in front of the massive three car garage. The house itself was lit up, both inside and out, illuminating its Mediterranean-like structure. It looked like it belonged in Cannes, overlooking the sea, rather than surrounded by tall oaks in Rustic Woods, Virginia. I especially loved the tile roof and wondered how they got that one past the Home Owners Association. A large donation of Ben Franklins to the pockets of HOA board members, guessed a cynical me.

Howard instructed me to drive past, then turn around and park on the opposite side of the road just far enough away not to be obvious, but close enough to easily view the house and the driveway. I turned the ignition off and glanced at the dashboard clock—9:15 p.m. We waited.

"So," I said. "you and me, alone, in a dark car. Maybe I wasn't lying to my mom. We could turn this into a date night." I put on a come-hither grin. "Of sorts." Wink.

He eyed me suspiciously. "You mean, steam up the windows? Then we couldn't see."

"Vision is overrated." I winked again.

"I think you have something in your eye," he teased.

"Just a twinkle for you, you hunk o' man, just a twinkle for you." I was leaning over jokingly for a romantic smooch, when he blurted, "Here we go," and reached under his seat retrieving a pair of binoculars.

"How did those get there?" I asked. It was my van, and binoculars were not part of my roadside emergency repair kit.

"I snuck them out of the house when your mother wasn't looking."

"We have binoculars?"

"I have binoculars."

Yes, he did, and his face was glued to them as we both watched a four-door sedan pull into the driveway. It motored slowly toward the garage and parked. Two people, a man and a woman, exited the car, met to join hands, and strode together down the long walkway leading to the front stoop. It didn't appear that they rang a doorbell or knocked and then waited to be greeted, but rather just walked right in. I glanced again at the clock on the dash: 9:20.

"Did they just walk in without knocking?" I asked of the man with a telephoto view.

"Yeah. Wasn't Shin Lee."

Five minutes later, another car, a Lexus crossover, pulled in and next to the first car. Another couple approached the house and walked in without knocking. A third car that arrived at 9:35 produced yet another hand-holding couple, but this time they knocked. I couldn't see, but Howard said it was a man who answered the door.

By 9:55, four more cars had arrived, all couples, some knocked or rang, others let themselves in.

Finally, I had to venture a guess. "Do you suppose that this is a," I made finger quotes in the air, "club meeting?"

"There's only one way to find out," he said.

"Are you serious? You want to walk into that den of iniquity?"

"You were just talking about gettin' jiggy wit it around a steering wheel."

"I wasn't inviting someone else to join us!"

"I can go alone."

"You'd look out of place."

"Then come with me. Everything Colt did leads us here. You'll be fine. You have your mace, remember. And I'm a human killing machine."

"Really?"

"No, but I'll watch out for you. You're my wife and the mother of my children after all."

"I'm not dressed for it. It looked like most of those women were wearing dresses."

"You look fine."

"Howard, this blouse is fifteen years old. It still has a stain from when I was breastfeeding Bethany."

"Breast milk stains?"

"No. I was trying to eat French fries and nurse at the same time. Ketchup dripped." I pointed. "See, right there."

"Are you stalling?"

I sighed. "What if no one finds me attractive?"

"I find you attractive, isn't that enough?"

"But if this is a swingers' party, other men should be looking at me, right? Isn't that how it works? Couples trading partners?" I shook a finger at him. "And you, by the way, are not allowed to look at other women." I slipped out of my jacket. If I was going to pretend to be a swinger, the ten-year-old fading and pilling fleece just wasn't going to cut it.

"I haven't looked at another woman since I first laid eyes on you in the campus library."

"Well now you're just being silly."

"No, I'm not. It's the truth." He kissed me softly, sweetly. "Now, come on, let's go." He opened the door, walked around the front of the van, opened mine, and took my hand.

I instantly noticed something was missing. "Wait, where's your cane?"

"It's getting in the way. I'm fine."

"It was part of the deal—you bring your cane, remember?"

"And you were supposed to bring your mace, but I happen to know it's in that jacket you just took off."

I narrowed my eyes at him, but gave up the fight. If we were, in fact, walking into a burrow of wife swappers, a cane and mace might be a bit extreme for fending off advances.

The long walk across the street and up to the front stoop was chilly and more nerve wracking than the hours leading up to a root canal.

Howard pushed the doorbell while I practiced exercises to prevent hyperventilation.

A tall, big-boned man with strawberry-blond hair and freckled cheeks opened the door. "Hello!" he said in a boisterous voice. His smile was genuine. "Are you new?"

"That's us," I quipped, "New, new, new." My voice cracked from nerves and I hoped the man hadn't noticed.

He lowered his voice to a near-whisper and leaned in as if sharing a secret. "You got the invite?"

Uh oh.

We did not anticipate the need for an invitation. One needed invitations for these things? I gulped. Okie dokie, how could I quip us out of this one?

Luckily, I had a husband with smarts and training from the best of the best, which usually referred to Top Gun School, but in this case referred to the FBI Academy. Smart Hubby Howard pulled the business card out of his back pocket and handed it to the friendly fellow who took the card with a wink and let us pass.

To our right was a massive living room. I mean, massive. You could fit five of my living rooms into that space. The furnishings were right off the cover of House Beautiful, including a shiny black baby grand piano in the back corner.

To the left, another living room. Two living rooms? To be fair, though, this one was smaller and had a television as well as a stereo system Howard would have killed for, I am sure.

Straight ahead through a wide hallway we could see a kitchen island the size of Maui and the hint of a dining room beyond. A few people milled around the kitchen island, preparing plates of food. I did not see Shin Lee anywhere.

For no other reason probably, than that we're both right handed, Howard and I slipped into the living room on the right and immediately caught the attention of a young couple standing with drinks in their hands. I tried to look down and avoid eye contact, but it was too late. The shortish brunette man smiled broadly and held his hand out for an introductory shake while the woman seemed more bashful.

"Name is Bob," he said. "This is Betty."

Betty and Bob? They didn't look a year over thirty, yet their names were at least sixty years old. "I'm Barb," I said taking his firm hand with my sweaty one. I cleared my throat. Boy, did I need a glass of water bad. "This is my husband, Howard."

I'm not sure if it was my imagination run amok, but I sensed Bob sizing me up. *Alright,* he was thinking, *Betty, Bob, and Barb, a threesome of Bs.*

"Barb!" bellowed Bob. "We've been expecting you."

Oh no! He *was* sizing me up. I grabbed Howard for support. This was heading in the wrong direction far too quickly. We needed Shin Lee, not a romp in Pee Wee Bob's Playhouse.

Bob peeked around as if checking out my rear end. "Where's the tequila?" he said, grinning.

I thought I might faint when the doorbell rang and a second later the kitchen erupted in joyful shouts of, "Barb! Finally! Barb!"

Spinning toward the door, my eyes landed on a face I never expected to see in a million years. Dandi Booker—all four feet of her. Her dyed blond hair was semi-teased into some style that I assumed was supposed to pass for sexy. It just looked like squirrels had nested there instead. She wore a low-cut dress so brightly orange that it could burn retinas, and she had her boobs all pushed up tight into a vice-like bra to give the illusion of cleavage. Yeah, I thought, when that thing comes off tonight, some man is going to be *very* disappointed.

"Hey, ya'll!" she cheered, all cheerleaderish. "Ready for some fun and margaritas?" She bounced a few times while lifting a party-sized bottle of tequila high into the air for everyone to see. I nearly expected her to break out into a chant: Give me a T, give me an E, give me a Q...

Bob turned his smile upside down. "You said *you* were Barb." His tone was accusatory.

"I am," I said, very confused.

Betty and Bob exchanged disappointed glances and walked off in what I detected was a huff. Our first rejection. I didn't know if I should be relieved or embarrassed. I thought about sniffing my pits to make sure my deodorant was still working, but reconsidered.

I whispered to Howard. "I know that woman, and her name isn't Barb."

"Who is it?"

"That's the friend-stealer, Dandi Booker. I can't wait to tell Peggy about this."

"I thought you didn't like gossips."

"That's not gossiping. That's telling the truth. I'm here, and so is Dandi, pretending to be someone else—me. If that's not a good truth to spread, I don't know what is."

My phone rang while Howard was rolling his eyes at me. I slipped it from my purse, trying to look casual. "It's Clarence," I told Howard.

He pointed. "I'm going to wander into the kitchen. See what shows up there."

I gave him a thumbs up and answered, moving into the far corner of the room, away from the voices that made it hard to hear. "Clarence, are you there?"

"Yeah. Hey, so we spent all afternoon researching this Saturday Night Fever and eventually Guy wound up on a discussion board and found out all kinds of cool stuff. This club has its own jargon and they refer to their parties as dances and guess what? They're having one tonight!"

"I know. I'm there right now."

"Really? So are we."

The doorbell rang.

"Clarence, what did you say?"

The boisterous, freckled guard who had answered the doorbell yelled out for the house to hear, "Hey! We got two gay guys!"

A resounding round of positive hoots and hollers echoed from every corner of the place.

"They don't have an invite, should we let 'em in anyway?"

More hoots and hollers and "Alright!" and "Show 'em the way!" and "It's cool to be gay!"

I was hearing this from both the house and the phone in my ear, so I knew the guys at the door were queer, but not gay. Pounding across the never-ending living room to the front door, I spied the long and stringy haired, younger version of Colt smiling proudly next to the pointy-nosed, fedora topped Guy Mertz who looked like a deer wishing he'd been caught in some headlights instead of caught in a possible panty parade.

"What are you doing here?" My tone was possibly a tad too motherly.

"It was his idea." Clarence pointed to Guy whose complexion had gone from red to green.

"Thought it would make a great story," stammered Guy whose eyes darted around. "But I'm starting to have second thoughts."

Clarence was beaming. "We're their first gay couple."

"Except you're not gay," I reminded him.

He shrugged. "It's still nice that they don't discriminate."

Pointing toward the far corner, I barked an order. "This way."

Across from the baby grand piano were two chairs. I motioned for them to sit and handed my phone to Clarence. "Here—look at your dad's last text and try to decipher. I'm getting Guy a glass of water." I snapped my fingers in front of Guy's face. "Stay with us. I'm getting you something cool to drink." He smiled weakly, taking the hat off his head and nervously fiddling with its brim.

Half way to the kitchen I bumped into Dandi Booker. I bumped into her hard, and I'll admit, I did it on purpose.

"Hey there, girl!" she chirped all Southern-like. She wrapped her hand around my arm and gave it a gentle squeeze. "Imagine finding a nice girl like you in a place like this."

"Why are you using my name?"

"What?"

"They called you, Barb. Your name isn't Barb. My name is Barb."

"Shh, girl, shh. Didn't anyone tell you the rules?"

When my face didn't register understanding, she sighed a deep Scarlett O'Hara sigh. "We don't use our real names here, for cripes sake. Everyone picks a name—you know a plainish name like Mary, or Sue, or Jane. Only those were already taken, so I took Barbara. Around here, I'm Barbara Haynes. Like the undies, but with a 'y' for spice." She put on a conspiratorial face. "I have to shake it up a teensy bit. It's just not in me to be all the way plain, you know? You should pick one quick-like. How about...Linda?"

"Barbara isn't a plainish name," I countered.

She patted me on the hand. "Oh, Sweetie, it works on you. Don't worry. How about Linda Miller?"

"Yeah, yeah, that'll do. Listen, I'm looking for the woman who I think lives here—Shin Lee?"

"You just don't catch on, do you? Club names, Linda, club names."

"Let's put it this way, anyone around that looks like her name could be Shin Lee? Who *lives* here?"

"That's Cathy Black, only I haven't seen her pretty little head yet tonight. She might be downstairs." She passed me a wink. "Some like to get started early, you know."

I winced as my mind darted toward images her comment conjured. Downstairs was probably where the "dancing" occurred. I couldn't even watch movies on Cinemax, aka, Skin-amax, so I sure as heck didn't want to catch the live show. But the fact of the matter was, Colt was in trouble and Shin Lee could be the answer. I asked Dandi-Barb where the stairs were. She pointed to a door off the hallway just past the far end of the kitchen.

More people had arrived, and even the mini-palace was starting to feel crowded. I scooched around and squeezed through small groups of chatty members until I reached the door. Above it was a lit blue and white neon sign that read, *Saturday Night Fever*. Beneath the words hung a pair of kissing lips, just like the business card logo. Man, these people were organized.

Pulling the door open revealed a nice surprise. Shin Lee the crazy Asian lady stood barefoot on the plushy carpeted stairs that did not go straight down, but rather made a bend half-way. She seemed to be talking to someone around the corner, obscured by the wall. Her silky blue and white dress fell just above the knee, but the neckline plunged nearly to her navel.

"You can do it, I know you can," she cooed in a gentle, very American-sounding voice. "You're the Master, baby, you're the Master."

So, she spoke English after all, that little faker.

Chapter Ten

My first impulse was to run for the hills, fearful I was about to witness a raunchy moment between two thrill-seeking suburbanites. However, my second impulse, which was to open my big fat mouth, overpowered the first, as it often does. "Hey, Miss No-Speak-English! What's the deal?"

That got her to notice me.

"You're the lady from this morning," she said, again, speaking better English than Colin Firth and Lawrence Olivier combined. "What are you doing here?"

With a great deal of courage that surprised the heck out of me, I stomped down the five or six stairs between us, peeked around the corner and said to the man in baggy jeans standing there, "Excuse me, I have some important business to discuss with your...uh... partner." I grabbed Shin Lee Cathy Black and pulled her up the stairs. "You have some 'splainin' to do," I told her.

"Get your hands off me. I'm not done with him yet."

"Really do *not* want to know the details, thank you." I gripped her arm tighter and kept pulling. "What's with the pretense that you don't speak English?"

She pulled back, but not hard enough to escape my grasp. "It's a time saver. I had somewhere to be. And you had a crazy look in your eyes."

I didn't know how she could have perceived my look as crazy, but I wasn't going to go there. "Cheap trick," I huffed.

"Who are you?" She seemed very angry with me for interrupting her debauched merger.

"Barbara Marr, Colt Baron's friend. You'd know that if you'd have given me half a second." I dragged her through the kitchen, into the living room and right up to Clarence and Guy, who were huddled together. Clarence was still holding my cell phone and Guy was scribbling notes on a ninety-nine-cent pocket note pad.

I presented them with a task. "This is Shin Lee, code name, Cathy Black. Don't let her fool you, she speaks English just fine. We saw her knocking on Colt's door this morning and we found a business card in his condo with this address on it. We suspect he was working for her since we found pictures of an Asian man on his camera from yesterday morning." I threw an apologetic glance to Shin Cathy. "Sorry if that sounds like racial profiling." I pointed to my "gay" friends. "This is Clarence, he's Colt's son, and just as worried about him as I am. And this is Guy Mertz. If you watch Channel 10, you've probably switched to another station when he came on. Put your hat back on, Guy, so she knows it's you."

The three of them were speechless, but Guy slipped his hat on anyway.

"Guy, get as much information from her as you can. I'm going to find Howard. I want to get out of this place before things get too weird." I was about to leave when I remembered something. "There were also pictures of a blonde in black sweatpants who we think is a woman named Rita Ash."

Clarence held up the phone for me to see. "Your friend Peggy called."

I turned on my heels to make an organized sweep for Howard.

"Barb, can you get me that water?" called Guy.

Right, the water.

As I passed by a man in a gray striped shirt, he asked, "You're Barb? Did you bring the tequila?"

I frowned. "That's Barbara Haynes. With a 'y' for spice." I made the sign of a 'y' with my arms raised. "Look for a midget that can do the splits." I shook my head, feeling bad for using that word. "I mean a vertically-challenged Southern drunk that can do the splits."

In the kitchen, I interrupted two women talking enthusiastically about some guy named John. "Excuse me, where could I find a glass?" I asked them.

The two women shared she's-so-dense sneers while pointing to the towel lined counter smack-dab in front of me loaded with clean hi-balls and wine glasses. The urge to stick out my tongue at them faded as my attention drew to a woman standing near a slightly opened pair of French doors that led outside. She was having a conversation with someone on the other side of the doors, but looking at me.

"That's not Barb," said the woman. "Barb's in the other room." She saw me zone-in on her conversation with the mystery person outside. "Hey!" she motioned me closer. "What's your name?"

"Uh..." What was it again? Oh, that's right. "Linda," I said with less confidence than a politician claiming he won't raise taxes.

"See, that's Linda. I told you, Barb is in-"

The double French doors flew open and Peggy appeared between them, angrier than I'd ever seen her. I actually think the red hair on her head was flaming. Literally, not figuratively.

Peggy wasn't the kind to get angry. When people flipped her off for driving too slow on the freeway, she felt bad for them because they weren't stopping to smell the roses. When people cut in line at the movie theater, she smiled and offered them her extra coupon for half-off a bucket of popcorn, simultaneously advising them to forgo the fake butter—it was rancid last time she was there.

"Barb, can I speak to you out here," she managed to spit through gritted teeth. "Please?"

I nodded, guilt-stricken, and followed her out as the irritated woman mumbled under her breath, "I wish people would either stick to the code names or drop the stupid game altogether."

When I stepped out, the cold air bit me good. It had dropped a few degrees since Howard and I arrived. I hugged myself for warmth. "What are you doing here?"

"I was running an errand and saw your van parked on the street. Have you listened to any of my messages? I've been trying to reach you."

If it had been anyone else, I would have been suspicious of the "running an errand" line, but late night jaunts were par for the Peggy's course. And as for dropping in on a party uninvited—when Peggy had a mind to do something, nothing stopped her.

"Yeah, I know." My gaze fell to the deck below our feet. "I've been busy—Colt's missing and I've been worried sick about him. Howard and I are here trying to get some information from a woman we think hired him for his last job."

Her face dropped. "That's terrible!" She hugged me tight. "I'm *so* sorry! I'm a terrible friend for yelling at you just now. Can I do anything? I can-"

There she went, offering me that half-off coupon, when deep down I knew that I was the bad friend here and if I let her continue apologizing, I'd be the worst friend ever. Worse than Patrick Swayze's embezzling bank buddy in *Ghost.* Although, I was really pretty sure I'd never hire a guy to kill Peggy and even if I did, I'd bet dollars to donuts that her ghost couldn't get mad enough to kill me back.

"No," I said, signaling her to stop. "I have a confession to make." I took a deep, cold breath. "I've been avoiding your calls, and I haven't listened to your messages, and it hasn't been because of Colt."

She looked as hurt as I thought she would. "He's not missing?"

"No, he's missing," I said. "But I was mad at you before I knew anything was wrong."

"The wine?"

I nodded. "And not just the wine. I've been jealous of Dandi Booker because..." I had a hard time saying the rest because it sounded so high-school petty.

Interestingly, Peggy finished the sentence for me. "Because she's an itch with a B up front, that's why. You were right about her. Not nice. Not nice at all."

Peggy had just given me the ammunition I needed to launch into my Dandi Booker tirade. "She's here and she's using my name!"

"I thought I saw her car. You have to be kidding me." She peeked back in through the doors. "Whose party is this anyway?"

It was getting far too cold to continue this gab fest outside. I pulled her into the house, closed the doors behind us and whispered, "This isn't a party like most parties," I said, thrilled to be sharing the darkly fun and dirty side of my evening. I grabbed two highballs from the counter, threw a few cubes from the ice bucket into them and handed her one. "Here, pretend like you're drinking while we talk. This is gonna get good."

"What kind of party is it?" she whispered back.

"It's a *sex* party."

Her eyes widened and she lowered the glass unconsciously.

"Glass back up. You're drinking, remember," I said, whispering over my own highball disguise, which, when I really thought about it, was a bad disguise since it was just a glass of ice.

She raised the fake drink back to her lips. "I don't see anyone having sex," she whispered.

"It happens downstairs. That's where people get freaky, if you know what I mean. This is a meeting place for swingers."

"No!" She was appropriately shocked. Her eyes scanned the room. "But why is Dandi here? She's divorced. I thought swinging was for married couples."

Hmm. I hadn't thought of that. She was right.

"And look," her eyes pointed behind me. "That's Rick, our soccer coach from last year. He's a widower." Her eyes landed on someone else. "And that's Nancy Whittier, I know she's single. Her husband left her two years ago for a hermaphrodite."

Suddenly, music was blaring in our ears and the room broke into cheers. Someone yelled, "The sound system is finally operational folks, and the dance floor is open!"

Peggy looked up at one of the speakers just above our heads. "That music is familiar," she said.

I nodded. "'Disco Inferno' from *Saturday Night Fever*." A shiver ran down my spine. "Are they going to orgy to Disco music? This is worse than I thought."

Peggy was doubtful. "I think they're just going to dance, Barb."

The house lights dimmed and little lights began to flicker on the walls and ceiling all around us.

"Oh look!" she pointed at the ceiling. "Little disco balls! How fun."

"Dancing is just a code word, Peggy. They have code names too. Dandi's code name is Barbara Haynes."

She wrinkled her nose and imitated a brilliant southern drawl. "Like the undies but with a "y" for spice?" She poked her finger into her mouth like she was inducing a vomit.

"How did you know?"

"It's her maiden name." Her hand curled into a fist. "She screwed me good, that one." She pointed behind me again. "There's Howard."

He'd spotted us and was trying to make his way through the flow of depraved sex addicts dashing for the basement. Just behind him were Clarence, Guy, and Shin-Cathy, who looked very annoyed.

Howard gave Peggy a nod of acknowledgement along with a raised eyebrow. I'm sure he wondered how she found me. He didn't vocalize his curiosity though. "I caught up with Martin and Lewis questioning Shin Lee. This isn't a swingers' club," he said. "It's a dance club."

"Told you," said Peggy.

"Then why all the code names and invites and secrecy?"

Guy spoke up, "She can tell you that." He gave Shin a little push and she threw him a dirty look.

"It's just part of the fun. We like to pretend it's something a little racy. You know, for the thrill of it. Plus, it's Disco. Some of us have reputations to uphold, you know?"

I set my chilled glass on the counter beside me. "But what about the discussion boards?"

She shook her head. "I've seen those, but they're getting us confused with a group out in Ashburn Heights. Now from what I hear, they *are* swingers."

Clarence laughed. "You guys should switch to Eighties music. Everyone thinks New Wave and Punk is cool."

Shin smirked. "That's Burning Down the House. They meet on Fridays in Oakton Park."

"Anyway," said Howard, slightly annoyed. "Shin did hire Colt to spy on her husband, who isn't here tonight."

She nodded, looking pained. "He said he'd be late. Again. You know, this is very personal. Do we need to be sharing it with the world?"

He continued, "Because she thinks he's having an affair with a club member named Rita Ash."

"Wait," said Peggy. "How long has Colt been missing?"

"The last time anyone saw him was yesterday afternoon," I said.

She crossed her arms. "That's weird. Really weird."

"Why?" I asked, starting to tire of the flickering lights from the disco balls.

"I just remembered that I talked to him yesterday afternoon. I saw him walking on the sidewalk when I was dropping one of the boys at a friend's house on Nectarine Drive. You know the kid, Barb. He's in Bethany's class. Nathan John or John Nathan and I have no idea which because my Daniel just calls him "Buddy," so I'm never sure if the mother's name is Jennifer John or Jennifer Nathan. Do you know which it is?"

"No." I gritted my teeth. "Anything else about Colt?"

"Oh. Right. He asked if I knew Rita Ash."

CHAPTER ELEVEN

Howard's face tightened with that bit of news and then his cell phone rang. He excused himself to take the call outside on the deck.

Shin Lee narrowed her eyes at the mention of Rita Ash. "Listen, I'm sorry I didn't help you earlier. Been in a mood lately. But I'm the hostess here. I need to get downstairs and make sure everyone is having a good time."

I looked to Clarence and Guy. "Did she give us what we need?"

Guy held up his note pad. "It's all here. She doesn't seem to know much. Howard could tell you better, but my hunch is we really need to talk to the husband."

I shrugged my shoulders at her and she scooted away. At the basement door, she turned back briefly. "I hope Colt is okay," she shouted above the music. "He's a good guy."

"Sounds like we really need to talk to Rita Ash too." I turned my attention back to Peggy. "Do you know her?"

She shook her head. "Nope."

That was unusual for Peggy. She usually knows everybody or at least knows someone who knows someone.

"But my cousin Aidan knows Rick," she added.

There you go.

"He owns those sports bars, Big Score Bar and Grill. There's one on Rustic Woods Parkway over on the North Side."

"Never been there," I said.

"Aidan's in the beverage supply business and says Rick Ash is probably going under soon. He dumped a bunch of money to open a second one somewhere in Western Fairfax, near the river, but I've heard that's not going very well. He's so far behind in his bills to Aidan that he'll have to cut him off soon."

Guy spoke up. "Do you mind if I ask a question?"

"Go for it," I said, chewing on the Rick and Rita Ash connection.

He cocked his head toward Peggy. "Who is *this* woman?"

"Guy, this is my friend Peggy. Peggy, Guy Mertz, true crime reporter."

She shook his hand. "I watch your news channel every night just hoping you'll have a new story to report. I love the dramatic flair you add. Did you study theater?"

He removed his hat, placed it over his waist, and took a bow. "Why yes, I did. Thank you for noticing." Returning the hat to his head, he asked. "And since curiosity is what brought me to news reporting, I must ask, why, exactly are you here?"

Peggy might have answered if Howard hadn't interrupted by opening the door into her. "Sorry Peg," he said. "Let's go, Barb. Eric sent a patrol car to the Ashes's, but no one answered the door. We're meeting him at a restaurant in North Rustic."

"Big Score Bar and Grill?" I asked.

He raised an eyebrow. "How did you know?"

"Simon is probably wondering where I am with that gallon of milk," said Peggy. "You could follow me to my house, I'll drop off the milk, then ride with you guys."

"We'll follow, Clarence will drive," said Guy. "I'm a man of the District. Bright lights, big city. The suburbs make me dizzy. It's so dark out here, I don't know how anyone finds their way around."

Guy did have a flair for the dramatic. Washington, D.C. was hardly a strobing metropolis like New York City. Although it *was* better lit than Rustic Woods.

Clarence snorted. It was his signature quirk. He had a lot of quirks, but his snort-laugh trumped them all. "Huh, yeah, I'll drive." He snorted again. "Like, it's my car." He leaned over and handed me my phone. "Take this before I drive off with it."

Howard's forehead had nearly collapsed on itself from frowning so deeply. He took my arm and pulled me into the dining room. "Can you call off your entourage?"

"Your voice has that testy quality to it again. What's wrong?"

"Nothing. I just want to get moving, minus Huey, Duey, and Screwy."

"Hey, she's my friend, watch what you call her."

He rolled his eyes. "Barb, come on. This isn't a game." His hand moved toward his knee, but stopped.

I narrowed my eyes at him. "How badly is your leg bothering you right now?"

"It's not that bad, now let's go."

He was fibbing. I can smell a fib a mile away since I try so hard not to commit them myself. "Maybe I should take you home and I'll meet Eric."

Right. As soon as the words hit air I knew that plan wasn't going to work. He cocked an eyebrow at me that said as much. I dug a bottle of Advil out of my purse. We went everywhere with Advil these days. It worked best when the pain set in. I told him to take two and showed him where the glasses and sink were.

As for "my entourage," as Howard referred to them, Clarence was too worried about his father so I wasn't going to send him home; Guy had nowhere to go without Clarence and his car; and I certainly wasn't going to say "no" to Peggy after I'd just apologized for being so dismissive of her.

"Okay," I whispered, turning back to them. I pointed to Clarence and Guy. "You two follow Peggy to her house, then she'll ride with you. Peggy, give them directions to Big Score. Now scoot!"

Clarence looked like he wanted clarification, or maybe a hug, but I shooed him away. "Meet you there. Scoot! Scoot!"

They were walking out the door by the time Howard returned, drugged up and ready to go himself. "Thank goodness," he sighed noticing the troublesome trio had departed. "Three less distractions on our plate."

I nodded. "Couldn't agree more." Well, I *did* agree. I wasn't necessarily abiding by his wishes, but I did agree with him.

We were halfway down the driveway headed back to my van when a stretch limo pulled in and slowly passed us.

"Someone important?" I wondered out loud.

Howard slipped his hand into mine while sneaking a glance back at the long black car. "I overheard a couple talking about a special mystery guest. They seemed pretty excited."

We kept walking, but my mind wandered to the snippets I caught between the two sneering ladies at the kitchen counter. They'd been awfully enthused and titillated about that guy named John. Of course, that's when I thought they were wives on the prowl for new meat. Now I wondered, could it be? No, that would be too far fetched. When I turned back around for a curious peek, a tall, robust man was walking toward the front door, escorted by two larger, even more robust men. Bodyguards? His hair was dark and the build seemed right.

I shook Howard more violently than I should have. "Look!"

He did, and when the door opened, freckles the invite man shouted a name that was hard to discern but had a ring of familiarity.

"Did he just say, Mr. Travolta, or was that my silly imagination?"

"It was your silly imagination," he said. "Probably." He pulled me across the street. "We have a friend to find."

And as we drove off, I couldn't help wondering: Did I just miss my chance to boogie with the Dancing King?

Howard drove to Big Score while I re-jacketed and warmed my hands on the dash heat vents. On the way, Howard filled me in on two little discoveries he made at the disco soiree. First, Shin Lee's husband was in fact the man in the pictures as she had admitted, but more interestingly, he was also the Dr. Kyung Kong of NOVA Urology, the practice Colt had visited for an exam. Secondly, Howard had found an envelope that looked very much like the one Rita Ash had handed to Dr. Kong in that picture Colt had taken. An angry Shin Lee gave him permission to take it. He'd tucked it in the back of his pants and under his jacket to keep it hidden in case Kong showed up before we left.

When we stopped at a red light, he leaned forward, wiggled it from under the back of his jacket, and handed it to me. "I didn't have time to look at it carefully," he said, "It appears that Rita and Kong were conspiring to do some business related to a found treasure."

"A found treasure?"

"You heard me."

"But it's so cool to say: found treasure. Are we talking like sunken ship kind of booty?"

"Booty?"

"Don't question my lingo, fork over the facts."

"Civil War-era gold."

"That's my luck. I'm tripping over dismembered members while someone else is discovering lost gold." I let the information sink in while the puzzle pieces began to click into place. "Didn't Eric say that the farmer guy had a disagreement with the Ashes? Maybe it has something to do with this treasure."

"Possibly."

I looked at the clock. Eleven thirty at night. The last time anyone had seen Colt was yesterday afternoon. "What about the Ashes' house? Can't the police search the place? We know he was following Rita. I'll bet he found out about the gold somehow, they were on to him, and they...kidnapped him maybe?"

"The police can't search their house. The wife who mentioned them in connection to her missing husband hasn't actually shown up to identify the remains. The report she made was over the phone so the names have to be verified in person before Fairfax County could have the authority to act. I think that's why he wanted us to meet him at the bar. Not sure, we didn't talk too long."

He pulled into the strip mall parking lot, the brightly lit sign welcoming us to Pine Bark Plaza. I knew of the plaza only because they had a mattress store where I bought a new box spring for Amber's bed when she broke hers playing "Kangaroo". Big Score Bar & Grill was two stores to the left of Mattress Heaven.

"They're still open?" I asked. "It's almost midnight."

"It's a bar and a restaurant, so I'm sure they stay open later for the bar clientele."

"We're so old, aren't we? Thinking midnight is late."

His voice went all crackly impersonating an old man. "I know, it's already three hours past our bedtime, Edna."

"Geez," I giggled, "I didn't know I married Rich Little."

Eric had been to our house during off-duty hours before, so I recognized his personal cruiser—a black Honda Accord. Howard parked in the empty spot next to it. Once inside, I was surprised by the absence of a host or hostess to greet us, but Eric waved his hand from a booth in the far left corner and we found our way without assistance. Or a menu.

The place wasn't rocking for a Saturday night, that's for sure. The establishment was broken into two sections: restaurant and bar. To the left were two rows of booths and to the right was a long, oak bar where a measly party of three men sat huddled over beers. Televisions lined the walls all the way around. There must have been twenty of them, all tuned to sports or news channels. Decor was definitely sports-oriented: framed football and baseball jerseys, pennants, posters, you name it. I wasn't overly impressed, but only because professional sports bore me to tears. I just really don't understand sitting for hours, watching a bunch of people I don't know, physically harm one another unless there's a decent plot involved. Or at least a couple crusty characters like Han Solo or Sam Spade to give the show some depth.

Only one couple sat in another booth two back from where Eric sat. If Peggy was right about Rick Ash having money troubles, it was easy to see why.

I slipped into the booth across from our friend of the law. Howard sat next to me. He took my hand in his, but spoke to Eric. "We're really worried about Colt," he said. "Something isn't right."

His words actually took me by surprise and warmed me all over. It was the first time he really expressed his concern. Maybe it was the FBI training, but the man didn't let cracks show in his armor. Not usually.

"I hear ya," said Eric. "Any more texts?"

Howard nodded and looked at me. "When was the last one?"

Pulling my phone out of my purse, I showed Eric the text.

"Twenty-one hundred hours," he read. He squinted, obviously trying to decipher the letters in the message. "Any idea what that means?"

I looked at the display again, myself, still baffled. "We haven't figured that out yet."

A bearded man yelled out to us from behind the bar. "Sorry for the wait! Be there in a minute to take your order!"

Eric scanned the room briefly, then leaned in closer, speaking more quietly. "Here's the thing. I did a little drive around this place before coming in. Rick Ash's truck is parked near the service entrance out back, so he's probably here."

"How do you know it's his truck?" Since he was off duty, I wondered how he managed that conclusion so quickly.

"License plates."

I nodded with a sense of understanding. "Had someone at the station run them?"

He shook his head. "They're personalized: RRASH."

Howard and I cringed in unison. Guess Rick Ash wasn't going for sexy when he thought up those plates.

"I haven't asked any questions, yet," said Eric. "Didn't want to raise any red flags too early. You want to run the show?" The last question was directed at Howard who nodded with a calm authority that aroused me slightly. He was so sexy when he took charge.

Mr. Facial Hair arrived a minute later, minus an order pad or a uniform as you often see on the wait staff of any restaurant or bar. He wore dusty jeans and a t-shirt bearing John Lennon's faded image. "Sorry, business is kind of slow tonight so I sent the bartender and head cook home. If you want something to eat, the only thing I can get for you are a few of the appetizers on our menu."

"Oh," said Howard, "the manager has to do all the work, huh?"

The man pushed out a sardonic half-laugh. "Manager quit. I'm the owner. What can I getcha?"

"I'll have a Corona," said Howard who then looked to me. "Barb, you want anything?"

"The same please."

Eric gave a nod, "Make that three."

"Three Coronas, coming up," said the man now positively identified as Rick Ash. "No appetizers?" he asked, already moving away to start on the order.

"Nothing, thanks," said Howard.

While he was gone, Howard slipped the envelope he'd taken from Shin Lee's house across the table toward Eric and whispered. "This is what I told you about on the phone," he said. "Careful he doesn't see it."

Eric took the envelope while keeping an eye on Ash who was too busy behind the bar to care what we were up to. He snuck a peek inside, taking a moment to read. "What's the Munson Treasure?" Then he flipped through a couple more of the pages. "Gold?"

"Looks like," said Howard. "From the Civil War. Here he comes."

Eric slipped the sheets back into the envelope, slid it onto the seat, and covered it with his jacket. Rick Ash was soon placing frosty, lime-topped, long-neck bottles in front of each of us. Howard said thank you, then added casually before Rick could move off, "So you're the owner, Rick Ash?"

The man nodded. "That's me."

"I'm Howard," he said, extending a hand for shaking. "You know a man named Orson Sparrow?"

Rick didn't hesitate to respond with a negative. "Don't know that name. Why?"

"He's a friend of mine. He told us about this place, I just got the impression you knew each other."

"Nope," Rick said shaking his head.

Howard turned to me. "Barb, didn't his wife say they knew Rick Ash? I swear she did."

Ash's response, which cut off my own role in this play, was too quick. "His wife?" he asked incredulously, as if he was surprised. He fumbled a minute, seeming thrown off balance, then added, "Who knows if I know the man. Or his wife. I meet a lot of people around here. Hard to keep track of names, you know? But tell him I said thanks for sending the business. Always appreciate that."

He gave a little wave and headed back the bar, but I'd swear he was sweating bullets under that facial overgrowth of his. He eyed us more warily from across the room.

"No reaction when you ask about Orson," I whispered, "but nervous wreck when you mention the wife? What's that all about?"

My phone rang. It was Peggy. I answered, wondering where they were. "Hey there. What's up?"

"We're not coming," she said.

That worked. I wouldn't have to explain to Howard why my "entourage" decided to follow us after all.

"Okay," I said. I was about to ask her what Clarence and Guy were planning but she beat me to it.

"I'm going with Clarence and Guy Mertz to Rick and Rita Ash's house."

CHAPTER TWELVE

U h oh.

"Who is it?" Howard asked.

"Peggy. She's with Clarence and Guy. They want to go to the Ashes's house."

"No, no," corrected Peggy when she heard me talking to Howard. "We're there now. We took a detour for a minute though—Guy thought he recognized the name of the street you said Colt's car was parked on. Sure enough. It's still there, and it's the next street over from the street the Ashes live on."

"We knew that already," I said.

"Tell them not to go anywhere near that house," urged Eric quietly. "We'll meet them there, but don't go on the property. We don't need that legal nightmare."

"Peggy, Eric says-"

"Guy deciphered the texts," she said interrupting me. "Here..." She must have handed the phone to Guy because his was the next voice in my ear.

"Barb, Guy here. I'd been working on the assumption that RM PT was short for *room point*, but that wasn't getting me anywhere. Then I called my nephew who suggested RM PT means *arm pit*. While this doesn't seem to make much sense either, if you look at the letters CHTG, and make the leap that Colt was off in his texting and he intended to key in an *r* instead of a *t*—they are just one letter apart on the keyboard after all—then it makes sense."

"What makes sense?"

"*Arm pit charge.* A couple of years ago I reported a story about this man who was hiking in some very isolated backwoods country when he fell down a steep embankment severely breaking his leg. He couldn't walk and his cell phone's battery was dead so he couldn't call for help. He removed the phone's battery and placed it under his armpit for several minutes. The heat gave the battery enough charge for the man to send an emergency text to his wife. Now, if we assume Colt is telling us that he is in danger, that he's been charging his cell phone battery under his arm pit, and his texts are emergency messages, then SOSND could be a distress signal and part of an address. The Ashes live on Nectarine Drive. ND."

I had to give it to him, that was pretty good investigative work. "That's excellent, Guy, but Eric says-"

I heard Clarence say, "That's not good," in the background, then Guy interrupted me again with a, "Gotta go."

CLICK.

"What was that all about?" asked Howard.

"They're at the Ashes's house because the Ashes live on Nectarine Drive—Guy thinks the code in Colt's text, SOSND, means he's there and in trouble." I waved my hand around. "And something about arm-pits and cell phone batteries. I think he's onto something. We should go, don't you think?"

While I had been relaying Guy's logic-play, Eric and Howard had shifted their attention to the entrance. Their eyes registered a sense of heightened alert, so I was careful to look as nonchalant as possible while trying to gaze in the same direction. I pulled my Corona up for a sip and simultaneously pivoted my neck just enough to see Dr. Kyung Kong flanked by two ultra-slim, immaculately suited Asian men. They moved directly to the bar and Rick Ash, seeming to anticipate their arrival, pointed to a location near the back wall where he proceeded himself. Kong and Ash spoke in hushed tones while Howard and Eric both raised their eyebrows.

"Is that what I think it is?" Eric asked Howard.

"The shorter one is Dr. Kyung Kong—the man I lifted that envelope from," he said, masking his moving lips with a pretend-swig of beer. "The other two are organized crime."

"You know them?" I asked.

Howard nodded. "Know of them. They're connected with a drug money laundering ring. Either they've left to work for Kong or he's been the boss all along. That house seemed suspiciously opulent even for a surgeon," he said narrowing his eyes. "Wonder what Ash has in that truck out back."

"Civil War-era gold?" offered Eric.

"Can't you call in the police right now?" I asked Eric as quietly as I could. "They're criminals, right?"

"I have to be careful what I do and don't do. There's no cause here yet. Just some guys hanging out in a bar. Wait and see what happens."

What happened was Rick Ash's voice rose louder and louder as the four men huddled. The three beer drinkers at the bar had turned their heads to observe the argument, but I still couldn't make out any words from where we sat. Eventually, Korean thugs One and Two broke away from the group. Their smart dress shoes clacked against the floor as they turned abruptly and headed toward the door. Ash and Kong exchanged a few more words, then Kong followed his friends.

The thrill factor was accelerating exponentially. First, a long-lost treasure of Gold from the Civil War days, then a urology surgeon who has sought financial reward from the seedy world of organized crime. Just when I thought things couldn't get any juicier, they did. Because just as those Korean mobsters were marching out the door, guess who ambled in? Or rather, *stumbled* in.

I couldn't believe my eyes. Again.

Dandi Booker. With a few too many margaritas in her, I suspected, by the wobble in her gait. Her eyes fell immediately on Rick Ash, whose face bore the look of a man caught in a trap. She stumbled in his direction, a venomous expression on her mascara-stained face, but then she swayed uncontrollably in the other direction and caught sight of me. Her eyes squinted as she attempted to focus in.

"Barb?" she slurred. "Ish that you, Barbara Marr, my buddy, my pal?"

Eric whispered across the table. "You know her?"

"Wish I didn't."

Dandi changed course and began tottering toward our table. I watched Rick Ash, whose eyes were glued on the entire scene. If body language was audible, his would be saying, "Holy crap, what do I do now?" I hadn't yet figured out why he was so concerned, but I thought if Dandi came any closer, I just might.

Eric shrugged back into his jacket, tucked the envelope underneath, zipped up, and leaned across the table. "This looks like a good time for me to break away and make sure your friends aren't breaking any laws." He threw a ten dollar bill on the table. "Meet me there."

Howard nodded an affirmative.

On his way to the front of the restaurant, Eric did some dancing in an attempt to avoid colliding with the teetering Dandi, but his footwork wasn't fancy enough and they crashed. Dandi craned her neck upwards like an average-sized pedestrian staring up the side of the Empire State Building.

"Ain't you a hunk o' handshome!" she gobbled. "I'll bet you're a real gentleman, huh?" She peered around him to give Rick Ash the evil eye. "Not like some two-timing, cheashing, shlime-ball, jerk-wad, lying, sonuvbishes I know!"

Eric didn't reply, but did put out a hand to keep her from falling over. Once she was semi-erect, he continued toward the door. Dandi floundered the rest of the way to our booth and careened into the seat across from Howard and me.

It looked like we were about to learn everything Dandi knew about Rick Ash, but somehow the prospect didn't cheer me. I was still worried about Colt, not to mention the three amateur sleuths who had apparently landed on something that "wasn't good." I checked my cell phone to see if there was a text from Peggy or Clarence – anything to let me know they were okay. Nothing.

Dandi didn't notice my phone check.

"Hi Barb," she said with a lopsided smile. "Ish thish your hubby?" Her breath reeked, and I thanked our lucky stars that Big Score didn't put candles on their tables. Otherwise, the fumes spewing off her breath would probably have ignited.

Howard was visibly tense. Across the room, Rick Ash pretended to wipe the bar down while stealing worried glances our way.

"Dandi," I said as kindly as I could manage, "would you like a cup of coffee?"

She put her chin in her hand and stared at Howard. "Anyone ever tell you how mush you look like George Clooney?"

Howard whispered in my ear, "Call her a cab."

She smiled, missing the whole thing.

"So," said Howard, leaning in, putting on a friendly face. "You're Dandi Booker?"

"Yeah, that's me. Dandi Booker. Or Barb Haynes, like the undies with a "y" at the Fever. I saw you there, you know. You're so cute. I wish I had a husband ash cute as you."

Dandi was falling into a nearly comatose state of inebriation. I got on the phone and asked the 411 service to redirect me to National Taxi.

"Dandi, why did you come here?" Howard asked. "Tell me quietly, so only I hear."

She licked her lips and rolled her eyes around. "He said he loved me. The grapes were gonna make it all better. Then they found the gold, but he still won't leave her." She seemed on the verge of crying.

Grapes? What the heck was she talking about?

"Sho you know what I did?" she continued. "I drove myshelf out to that farm." Her head flopped around. "Told Orson they took his gold, that'sh what I did." She sat back and sighed. "Sheemed like a good idea at the time."

She was taking longer and longer between sentences and I was growing annoyed. I tried not to show it though. "Anything else?" I asked, hoping to move things along.

"I felt bad, y'know?" She attempted to blow some strands of hair from her eyes and when that didn't work, she swiped at them angrily.

"I went back, but then he wasn't there anymore...so I called. Said I was his wife, Cherry. You like that name Cherry? I like it almost as much as Dandi, don't you?"

"By 'he,' you mean—and keep this very low, Dandi—do you mean Rick Ash?"

She nodded. Her heavy eyelids were at half-mast.

"And whose wife did you pretend to be?"

"Orson's," she sniffed.

Okay. So Orson Sparrow owned a farm. Possibly he grew grapes? I was wishing I could slap some serious sobriety into this woman so we could get a clearer story.

"Does Orson have a real wife?" asked Howard.

She shook her head, then raised her lids a tad. "Get me a Bloody Mary, would ya? I'm awful thirsty."

The room was emptying out. The couple who had been seated at a booth had left shortly after Eric, and now the men at the bar were leaving as well.

Rick Ash meandered our way, trying to look a little too aloof. He put a bill on the table and glanced at Dandi.

"I, uh, know the lady," he said. "I can take care of her from here."

"Thanks," said Howard, looking Rick straight in the eye. "But we've called her a cab. We'll make sure she gets home safely." He pulled a twenty from his wallet and threw it on the table with Eric's share. "Keep the change."

Appearing both annoyed and strained, Rick took the bills and left.

"What are we going to do?" I asked Howard. "Carry her out of here?"

"You take one side, I'll take the other," he said. "She can probably walk with our support."

I did as he said, and after some very awkward shifting of arms here and legs there, we managed to start her on a trajectory for the exit. I was happy to see the taxi pull up just as we reached the door.

"Barb," she said, blowing her tequila breath all over me. "You're sho lucky to have a George Clooney who's so nishe and schweet."

"Right, right, Dandi," I said. "I know. He's a George Clooney in a million."

She melted into the back seat of the taxi cab while Howard gave the driver money along with a stern order to treat her well. She had kids and a babysitter at home.

"Dandi," I said. "Tell him your address, okay?"

She worked hard to keep her eyelids from drooping. "Sure will, Barbie, sure will." Then she grabbed my blouse and pulled me so close to her face I thought we were about to have a Britney Spears and Madonna moment. "He hash a nickname, you know."

"Who?" I asked, although I was pretty sure I knew the answer.

"Ricky."

"What's the nickname?"

Her eyelids fluttered and her head flopped back onto the seat.

"Dandi," I urged. "What's the nickname?"

She hauled herself back up, cupped her hand around my ear and whispered, "'The Butcher.' They call him 'The Butcher'."

Chapter Thirteen

The taxi pulled off slowly while Howard and I stood on the curb wondering what to do next.

"She just told me that Rick Ash's nickname is 'The Butcher,'" I said. "That can't be good for Colt if he's caught up in this mess."

"Did she say why?"

"Did she need to? I'm betting Orson Sparrow, also known as The *Praçia* in the Woods, knows why."

He cocked his head as if giving that some thought. "Dandi riled Orson who went to the Ashes's looking for gold found on his land; the Ashes's killed him then butchered him." He paused. "Maybe."

Meanwhile, I had pulled out my cell phone.

"What are you doing?"

"Calling Peggy to see if Eric is there yet." I scrolled down to her name and tapped *call*. Seconds later I heard her message. I blew out a frustrated breath while ending the call. "Voicemail." Quickly, I tried Clarence's phone only to achieve the same result. This was beginning to feel all too familiar. "They're not answering. We need to get over there."

Howard put his sights back on the restaurant. "Eric can handle things there. You get in the car and lock the door. I'll be back in a minute."

"Where are you going?"

"Just to ask Ash a couple more questions."

"No! He's 'The Butcher,' remember?"

"Barb, I used to do this for a living, remember?"

"Yeah, until you almost died. *Remember?*"

I didn't like the idea in theory. It felt risky. And I was anxious to find my three amigos, praying they were safe, albeit silent. But Howard had a point—he and Eric were professionals. Certainly, Rick Ash wouldn't pull out a cleaver and chop Howard to bits in a public place without provocation. I relented, deferring to Howard's expertise.

"How many questions?"

"Two. Three tops."

"You'll be quick, safe, and smart?"

He put his hands on my shoulders and looked me in the eyes. Man, but he had dreamy eyes. "Always."

"Then we'll head over to the Ashes's house?"

"That's the plan."

We kissed and parted ways. Howard headed back into the bar, which Rick had not locked up yet. I walked toward my van, one of the last in the dimly lit parking lot. The only other was a sedan on the opposite end of the lot.

I fumbled in my purse. I could hear my keys rattling around, but it was too dark to see and my groping fingers couldn't locate them. I'd never liked being in a deserted parking lot alone, but I found it especially creepy when the accompanying establishment belonged to a man with a deadly nickname.

My hands finally locked around my key ring; at the same time, the lights of the sedan across the parking lot flicked on. I clicked the "unlock" button on the fob, but nothing happened. I muttered a curse word under my breath. I'd forgotten that the fob battery was low. An engine revved on the far side of the parking lot, and I noticed that the sedan was moving slowly in my direction. The click of a lock drew my attention to the door of the bar. Rick Ash stood inside, staring out at me through the glass door. His face was stone-hard.

Howard was in the bar. Why was Rick locking up if there was still a customer in the bar? Panic set in.

Without thinking twice, I started walking back toward the restaurant. Then I stopped, realizing that if Howard was in trouble inside the restaurant, maybe I should get my mace ready. Stopping to think turned out to be a mistake. While I was slowing down, the car was speeding up and was now making a beeline for my body. In a flash of a moment, two things happened: First, I recognized the license plate, FEEVRR, on Rita Ash's red Mercedes E550. Second, I decided to do what action heroes do when a car is about to mow them down—I jumped onto the hood.

I have been known to pass out on occasion. I wished that now would have been one of those times, because the crushing pain of impact was worse than anything I'd ever experienced—including childbirth and being struck by a bullet at close range while wearing a Kevlar vest. Unfortunately, I did not lose consciousness before, during, or after the whole horrific incident.

After colliding with the hood, I rolled onto the windshield, cracking my head against the glass. Then I rolled farther, across the windshield and almost onto the top of the car, which by now had skidded to a hard stop. Momentum flung me forward onto the cold, hard pavement, where I landed with a thud. I was far too dazed and confused to move. My entire body throbbed, my head pounded, and bile rose in my throat. The door of the car opened and for the first time I saw Rita Ash in person. She was still dressed in sweat pants, the same ones she'd been wearing in the pictures. Her blond hair was pulled back.

My vision began to blur. A moment later I felt myself being dragged and then lifted. Someone grunted in my ear. A few moments later the world began rocking, something like being on a boat.

Although I didn't actually lose consciousness, I did have a visit from Meryl Streep and Steven Spielberg. Usually this only happens when I'm dreaming, but apparently waking delirium was close enough.

We were in a limousine and Meryl was the driver. She had the black suit and little black hat and everything. Let me tell you, that woman looked stunning, even in her chauffeur's uniform. She could wear a dirty rug and make it look like runway style. I could see her eyes in the rearview mirror. Steven was seated in the other seat, facing me. His hands were clasped together, his elbows on his knees and he leaned toward me with a look of concern on his face.

The fact that I was in a limo with Meryl and Steven (that's what I call them, Meryl and Steven—I feel so cool) gave me goose bumps. I wondered whether we might be headed for my dream destination: The Academy Awards.

"Please tell me we're going to the Oscars," I said to Steven.

"It ain't good, Barb, it ain't good," he responded with a solemn shake of the head. He sounded more like Michael Corleone than Steven Spielberg.

"Steven, why are you talking like a Goodfella?"

"You gots a problem, here, y'know?" he continued, ignoring my question.

"Meryl," I pleaded, "Why is he talking like this?"

"A farm in Africa, I had," she began, not in her own voice, but that of Frank Oz's Yoda. "At the foot of the Ngong hills, it was."

So there I was, in a dream-limo, with an Italian Mafioso Steven Spielberg and Meryl Streep impersonating a Star Wars icon. If only we were on our way to a red-carpet walk, I thought, this dream would be so much more fun. But I couldn't tell whether we were Oscar-bound or not, since neither of them were addressing my questions directly. You'd have thought they were presidential candidates on the debate trail. I pressed forward for answers, or a possible way out to reality.

I offered a question to the both of them. "Why am I here?"

Steven threw up his hands. "You was run over by a car, don'tchoo remember nuthin'?"

Meryl seemed to be in her own world. "Knew, perhaps he did, that made round the Earth was," she kept reciting Yoda renditions of lines from *Out of Africa*, "so see down the road too far, we would not."

Or was she in her own world? It occurred to me there was a theme— Mafia Steven talked about the car and Yoda Meryl pontificated on "seeing down the road." Were they sending me a message?

"Are you speaking to me in riddles?" I asked, beginning to think I was onto a DaVinci's Code-esque set of clues. "Should I be digging deeper into the meaning of your answers?"

Steven rolled his eyes. "Nah," he said. "Meryl there is workin' wit a vocal coach, preparin' for her role as Yoda's wife in George Lucas' first pre-quel to the pre-quels to the Star Wars Saga." He called forward to her. "What's dat movie gonna be called again?"

Meryl dropped the Yoda voice. *"Star Wars, Episode A-1: With You, May the Force Be.* George is convinced he can erase Episodes One through Three from viewers' memories and regain the love of his fans with this newest trilogy which explains that Jar Jar Binks was just a really, really bad dream."

I cringed. "I knew I was upset that Disney bought Lucasfilm," I said. "But I never thought it would affect my hallucinations."

Steven shrugged, "Whatcha gonna do, right? If nuthin' else, they'll make their money back in DVD sales and merchandisin'." He leaned in close and furrowed his brows. "And I ain't Steven Spielberg, Barb. Ain't ya figured out who I am?"

The voice was familiar, now that he mentioned it.

"You're not Michael Corleone?" I asked.

"Heh, don't I wish? One day, though, I'd like ta meet Pacino, right? Here's a clue." Steven-not-Steven began to croon, "Come fly with me," just like Frank Sinatra.

Of course! How I didn't see it sooner, I didn't know. But as soon as I realized Steven-not-Steven was really my rehabilitated criminal friend, Frankie Romano, he transformed before my dream-state eyes. Frankie had once kidnapped me, but now we were tight, and looked out for one another.

"Frankie!"

"Yo, Barb," he said with a smile. "Good ta see ya, although, da circumstances are less than copasetic, am I right?"

"You hit that nail on the head."

"Listen, we ain't got much time, so I'll put it to you fast-like: dis broad, drivin' da car," he pointed to the front seat. "She ain't Meryl Streep. It's dat Ash chick and she's got brains smaller than an alligator's. Her husband too. Just remember, in dis, you got da upper hand."

"How about Howard? Is he okay?"

"Da thing is, I ain't real. Dis is just dream-Frankie, ya know?" He looked very apologetic, I must say. "I can only point out da tings you already know—on a subconscious level, dat is."

He sat back and pointed to my chest. "Oh, and one of those ribs might be broken. Nuthin' time won't heal when dis is all over, but, and dis is key, don't let anyone know yous hurt. Don't show da pain."

I nodded. "Don't show da pain."

He was starting to fade when I wondered, why? Why not show da pain? But he and Yoda-Meryl were gone before I could ask the question. Just like the movies, in life, dreams only reveal enough to move the plot forward.

I was awake when Rita Ash pulled her Mercedes to a stop. In my semi-conscious state, I missed the binding of my ankles and wrists. I now lay in fetal position in the backseat, with my bound hands near my face. I was able to see up through a sliver between the seat in front of me and the car door, and glimpse an outdoor lamp as it glowed from its secured location on a brick wall.

Rita opened her door just as I heard the approaching motor of another vehicle. I craned my neck enough to see that the new arrival was a large pick-up truck. The slamming of Rita's door and the crunching of her shoes on gravel was followed by discussion between a man and a woman. The voices were low and far too garbled for me to make out words.

Inspecting my wrists more closely revealed that my captor had used decorative package ribbon to tie me up. According to dream-Frankie, she wasn't a rocket scientist, and the curling ribbon bindings seemed to prove him correct. I pulled at the ribbon binding in hopes of loosening it before anyone had a chance to stop me. Unfortunately, not much loosening occurred before the door by my feet swung open and a large pair of hands grabbed my legs. I held my breath and braced myself, anticipating forced movement that would surely hurt like the dickens. Sure enough, the mystery hands tightened and yanked.

Oh man it hurt, but I successfully bit back the urge to yelp in agony. Another yank, and I was out of the car. A third, and I'd been hoisted onto the shoulders of possibly the hugest man on earth. I felt easily ten feet off the ground and since I was now near the top of him, looking down, I could see his backside was very wide as well. This guy, I decided, if he had a shred of acting talent at all, could easily play Lennie in yet another movie remake of *Of Mice and Men.* I just hoped I wouldn't go the way of that poor puppy or Curley's wife.

I turned my upside-down head a bit, working to see where I was. Rita was nowhere in my sights. I was, however, able to glimpse not one, but two trucks parked nearby. Lennie began moving and I bounced with each step. We were outside in what appeared to be the back of another strip mall. If it was a shopping center of any kind, I reasoned, and there were other people around, screaming might possibly save my life. On the other hand, screaming might incite the giant to squash me like a bug. I didn't have much time to decide because Lennie, despite his size, moved at a decent clip. Hoping beyond hope that someone somewhere would hear and rush to my rescue, I risked it and wailed away.

"Help!" Somehow the plea didn't sound loud enough. I gave it another go. "Help! Help! Someone help me!" I was shrieking now.

Lennie laughed. "You kin yell all yoo want outchere," he drawled in a deep Southern tone. "Ain't gonna do yoo one bitta good. We're in the middle-a gosh-darn no wheres."

Gosh-darn? Did he really say gosh-darn?

Not to beat a dead horse, but I had been kidnapped before, and always by people who liked a little more bite to their curse words. This, I had to say, was a refreshing change.

Gosh-darn Lennie grabbed hold of a metal door, pulled and ducked. I swear, I am not making this up. He was so tall he had to duck to get us both through the door. He did a pretty good job until the metal door swung closed so fast that it bonked me hard on the head.

"Sorry 'bout that," said the Hagrid-sized man. He turned, I guess to see if I was okay, but since I was on his back he just ended up banging my head on the wall. I was beginning to think I'd survived a collision with a Mercedes only to have my life cut short by unintentional brain-bashing.

"Oh," he said, "sorry again."

Afraid he'd continue throwing me into walls and other hard objects, I interjected. "That's okay," I croaked, grinding my teeth from the pressure of my broken rib pressed against this man's shoulder. "Just take me wherever you're taking me, please." The blood was starting to pool in my head, causing it to throb all the more.

Apparently, that wasn't far. In through one door we turned and voilà, there I was, on the shoulders of a giant, looking down at Peggy, Clarence, and Guy. They were bound hand and foot with duct tape, but only poor Peggy, for reasons I could guess pretty easily, had a big ol' piece slapped across her mouth.

CHAPTER FOURTEEN

Clarence's face brightened in what I read as relief when he saw me. Although I'm not sure why having me there was anything to be relieved about. Possibly he was happy to have another friendly face to die with?

Guy had a bruise on his left cheek and his head was hat-less. I wondered if he'd lost his precious fedora in a struggle. Poor Guy. He wasn't exactly equipped for violent encounters.

"You okay, Guy?" I asked as Lennie-Hagrid lowered me gently to the concrete floor next to Peggy.

"There have been times in my life," he answered, "that were far superior, emotionally speaking, than this particular experience, thus far. The question, I guess, going forward, is, will things get better or worse?"

Lennie-Hagrid chortled while lowering himself onto a stool near the opposite wall.

"Barb's here," noted Clarence, "so I'm saying better. Right?"

Guy released a mildly derisive grunt. "The problem with that logic is that Barb is here, and not elsewhere, seeking the assistance of law enforcement for our rescue. And, I might add, she looks like she's been run over by a Mack truck."

"Just a Mercedes," I said. "Do I look that bad?"

"You won't be taking a stroll down Project Runway anytime soon, let's put it that way," he answered. "Now, as long as her federally anointed husband is still at large, possibly there is hope for us yet."

Voices echoed in the hall outside our prison-room. Rick and Rita I was guessing. A moment later Howard appeared in the doorway, his hands above his head. He wasn't tied up at all. Geez, he wasn't bruised or beaten or anything. He limped very noticeably though, leading me to assume that he was not doing so well. Rick Ash appeared next, and even though I couldn't see it yet, I was pretty sure he held a gun to Howard's back.

Guy's head fell back against the wall, his spiky nose pointing to the unfinished ceiling above us. "That does it. We are officially doomed." He gave this a moment to sink in, then followed with, "Unless, by some miracle, we are saved. In which case, this will make one hell of a good story. Emmy-worthy, possibly. I've always dreamed of winning a local Emmy," he sighed.

"Over there against the wall," Rick instructed Howard. "But not too close to the others. And, uh..." he waved the gun around in circles like a gangster in a James Cagney movie. He was thinking. "Uh, sit on your hands. Yeah, sit on your hands."

Howard did as he said, slipping down to the floor against the wall a good six feet from Clarence. Rick stood in front of us, gun aimed in our general direction.

A small chuckle—which didn't seem so much happy as nervous—escaped from the man with the deadly gun. "I know you now," he said to Guy. "You're that freak show reporter on Channel..."

"Ten," assisted Guy. "Channel Ten. Local News at four and five. You might know my friend over there, as well—meet Clarence Heatherington, Channel Three's movie reviewer."

Rick Ash's face went from obliviously blank to stymied and mildly distressed. "Crap." He scratched his beard with his free hand.

He was a man of few words. And evidently not the most astute, which surprised me since he was a business owner. But, if what Peggy said was true, he wasn't savvy as an entrepreneur either. Thus, the lack of aptitude made more sense.

"You okay?" Howard asked, giving me a visual once-over. Bless him, those puppy-dog eyes expressed his worry more deeply than the question.

I would have loved to have shouted, "No! I need a doctor! Karate-chop this man with the gun and get me to a hospital quick!" but dream-Frankie said this would be wrong. *Don't show da pain.* I smiled weakly. "Doin' good," I said, "doin' good. The Mercedes though, probably won't make it through the night."

"What happened?"

"You didn't see?"

"Otherwise occupied at the time."

"Right. Well, your abductor's wife wanted to play bumper cars, only she played dirty and started before the buzzer sounded."

My butt was starting to ache, not to mention go numb from the hard, cold concrete. For the first time, I gave my surroundings some inspection. Our stockade, if you will, was a room probably about ten feet by fifteen feet. The walls were unfinished. It reminded me of how our basement looked before they sanded and painted the drywall when we had it renovated. In fact, a bucket of something was still sitting in one corner, as well as a dry sponge and a putty-knife. Electrical outlets and light switches were naked without covers, and on the wall ahead of me and behind Rick Ash, several dangling cords protruded from the wall—unused, unconnected. There was no ceiling to speak of, just open ductwork and darkness. A stack of ceiling tiles leaned against one wall indicated they had eventual plans to hide the ductwork. The only door led to a hallway with the same unfinished atmosphere.

Peggy had mentioned a second restaurant that wasn't getting off the ground. This might be it, although I had pictured an open establishment struggling to find clientele. This place was struggling to find a life. The Ashes's must have had a ton of money wrapped up in another Big Score that wasn't scoring them any monetary return at the present. Liquidating a long-lost Civil War-era treasure would probably go a long way in alleviating any financial stress.

I considered our captors. I'd already pegged Rick Ash as less-than-clever, but he had the gun and a scary nickname, so he wasn't to be dismissed. And Rita, while I hadn't had a chance to chat, had certainly revealed herself as lead-footed and willing-to-kill. But this giant man-boy, whose real name I hadn't yet learned, was sizing up to be kind and gentle and very possibly our ticket out of this joint, hopefully all in one piece rather than chopped into dog-tasty, bite-sized morsels like poor Orson Sparrow.

Rita returned, black sweat pants and all. She stood next to Rick, one hand on her hip, the other twirling strands of hair that had slipped out from the haphazard bun at the back of her head. She wore a surprisingly dirty pair of running shoes with a bright magenta stripe, a crusty blue t-shirt covered by an unzipped, darker blue hoodie, and I'm pretty sure she wasn't wearing a bra. Now, I understand that this wasn't very important to our dire circumstances, but she was the kind of woman who needed to wear a bra—who bras were invented for. Me, if I wear a bra, it's just for show, because the sad fact of the matter is, what little I have needs no holstering. But Rita Ash—her gallon milk jugs needed serious support. She wasn't wearing makeup, but she had features that suggested just a little would go a long way and somehow, she looked vaguely familiar now that I saw her up close, but I couldn't place how. Possibly we shopped at the same grocery store?

The two of them stood there, Rick packing his scruffy beard and 9mm menace and Rita with her menacing mammaries, not speaking, just looking at us like they'd look at a piece of furniture that didn't seem nearly as stunning in their living room as it did on the showroom floor.

"This is a mess," Rita finally sighed.

Rick raised his eyebrows as if surprised, but then just agreed, "A mess."

They eyed us several seconds longer. Then Rick turned on her. "What were you thinking, bringing those four here?"

She stopped her hair twirling to give him a glare. "It was your idea, remember?"

Silence again, and I was beginning to thank my lucky stars that my most recent captors did not seem very decisive.

"Five hostages!" She threw her arms into the air for emphasis. "Five hostages. What are we going to do with five hostages? I can just kiss that Happy Housewives gig goodbye. I was so close, too."

Aha! Now I knew who Rita Ash was and boy, she could clean up nice when she wanted to. A year earlier, she'd been involved in some big stink over a political fund-raising event held in the District. She claimed she had an invitation, but she wasn't on the guest list, and all annoyed and full of herself, she barged in anyway. The ballyhoo made national news, if I remembered right, and just a few weeks ago, I had seen a local news piece announcing she was being considered for the newest cast of Happy Housewives in D.C.. I couldn't believe Guy didn't pick up on this earlier.

"Guy," I said giving him an irritated glance, "how didn't you know who Rita Ash was?"

He shrugged. "Who is she?"

"The famous party crasher—you know, last year. Whose fundraiser was that?"

"Senator Williams," Rita said flatly. "I had an invitation."

Some sense of recognition lit on Guy's face. "Yes. I remember that story." He shook his head. "Falls under entertainment and I don't get those assignments nearly as often as I'd like. A chance to attend a premiere screening every once in a while, but my beat's mostly the killers."

"We're not killers," retorted Rita.

"Excuse me," apologized Guy. "I did not mean to imply that you were."

I seriously wanted to argue Rita's assertion that she wasn't a killer, since it sure did feel like she was trying to do me in with that car stunt.

"Actually," Rick said to Rita. "*We're* not killers, but *you* are. At least, by definition, right?"

Who were these people anyway?

"I told you it was an accident," she growled, her eyes blazing. "How many times do I have to tell you that?"

Rick let out a sardonic chuckle. "Right, and you had an invitation."

"I *did* have an invitation!" Rita's face flamed red.

Rick and Rita were not a happy couple. Probably a lot of stress there, what with all of the murdering, cleaving, and kidnapping. I wondered if Rita knew about his little Dandi dalliance.

While we were on the subject of hurting people, I decided to ask about Colt. Did I think it was likely they'd give me a straight answer? No, but at least I could watch their reaction.

"What did you do with my friend, Colt?"

Not the slightest tick of recognition registered on either of their faces. "Colt who?" asked Rita.

"Don't give me that. I know you're not that dumb. Blond PI who was following you yesterday." I pointed to Peggy. "The last time she saw him was on your street. Explain that."

The dissatisfied spouses exchanged blank expressions. "You know about this?" Rick asked Rita.

"No," she answered. "You?"

They seemed truly stumped. It was very hard to tell if they were playing me or not.

"I'm figuring he slipped into your house, found evidence you'd killed Orson Sparrow, so you took him hostage like you have us now. Is he still in your house? What did you do with him?"

Rita looked like she was on the verge of breaking into laughter. "Is that who she was babbling on about?" she asked, pointing to Peggy. She threw her hands in the air, seeming exasperated. "Oh my God, I can't believe this."

The conversation was becoming more confusing than a Fellini film. Guy read the blank look on my face. "I think I'm beginning to understand what is happening here," he said. "Let me explain." He wiggled a bit where he sat. "When we were...approached by this Rita woman initially, Peggy began to spill the beans, so to speak. In essence, she said that we knew the woman was keeping a man in the house, that he was Clarence's father, and that our friend Barbara and her husband were at Rick's bar at that very minute, to get some answers."

Rita started pacing and Rick just rubbed that beard some more. "Holy crap," he said finally.

Guy continued. "It would seem," he looked at Rita. "Correct me if I'm wrong. It would seem that our kidnapping is the direct result of a misunderstanding that we knew you had killed someone. Is it possible that you not only murdered a man, but that his body is still in your house?"

Boy, crime reporting pays off. Guy really could put things together.

"She killed him," Rick said. "I didn't have anything to do with it!"

"It was an accident!" shouted Rita.

I needed to confirm my own theory while we were at it. "It's Orson Sparrow, isn't it? You killed Orson Sparrow!"

Lennie-Hagrid began chuckling on his stool and I began to wonder if I'd misjudged his kind nature.

"What's so funny?" I asked.

"You think they kilt Orson Sparrow, that's what's so funny," he chuckled some more.

"I doubt Orson Sparrow thinks it's funny," I countered.

He just couldn't contain his chuckle. "They kilt someone alright, that's true enough, but it weren't no Orson Sparrow 'cuz Orson's right here in this room."

Of the five men in the room, I was sure three of them weren't Orson Sparrow. I looked at Rick Ash. Certainly, I'd had my run-ins with impersonators, but somehow I just didn't think he was going to tear off a mask and say, "Hey, there, I'm a grape farmer." That left one person. Lennie-Hagrid, the gentle giant. "You?" I asked him.

"That's right, yoo silly goof, me!" the big man bellowed, poking himself with a monstrous thumb. "I'm Orson Sparrow and I ain't dead."

CHAPTER FIFTEEN

And the plot thickened.

So, if Orson Sparrow wasn't "kilt," then whose *prącia* did I find in the woods behind my house? It was all getting to be too much with my rib cage aching and my head throbbing. On top of that, nausea was creeping up on me just a little too quickly for comfort. And we were no closer to knowing what had happened to Colt.

"I don't feel so good," I moaned, and leaned sideways until my head was resting on Peggy's shoulder. Poor Peggy had been gagged through all of this and tried desperately to communicate, but had finally given up. Now she hummed "Mmm mmm," which I decided meant, "Poor Barb."

Rita stomped out of the room and returned several seconds later with a huge wad of plastic grocery bags. She ripped the gun from her husband's hands and shoved the bags at him. "Tie him up," she said, pointing the gun in Howard's direction.

"With these?" he whined. "How am I going to do that?"

"Are you completely useless?"

Rick did as ordered and kneeled beside Howard, starting in on his wrists. Howard winced a few times.

"Maybe we could git the lady some soup or sumthin' if she ain't feelin' right," offered Orson.

Rita pinched the bridge of her nose between her fingers as if trying to relieve the pressure of a headache. "Orson. Go to the kitchen. We'll be there in a minute."

Meanwhile, Rick continued to tug and twist and tie until he felt satisfied that he'd eliminated any chance of Howard either hitting him or running away.

"I think it's cutting off my circulation," said Howard.

"Good," interrupted Rita before Rick could do anything about it. "That means you won't be going anywhere." She motioned to Rick. "Come on. We need to make some decisions."

We were left alone, although since there were five of us, that hardly felt alone. At least we were free to compare notes.

"Anyone have a cell phone?" Howard whispered.

"Miss Happy Housewife took ours," moaned Guy.

"Mine is in my purse. Which is in the back of her car. They're not entirely organized, but they're not the stupidest criminals in the world either."

"What do you think they're doing?" whispered Clarence. "Making a bomb?"

We all shot him a bewildered glare.

"Any ideas on how to get us out of here?" I asked Howard.

He pivoted his head, surveying the room. "Not yet. I'm working on it." He began pulling at his plastic bag binding with his teeth. That seemed like a smart idea, so I started to do the same with my ribbons, but Howard stopped me.

"No," he whispered. You keep talking. Act natural or they'll come back in."

I wasn't sure how natural I could act under the current circumstances, but talking I could do. I proceeded with my original plan: piece together the sequence of our kidnapping. Now we knew why: Peggy talked too much. But how?

"Guy," I said, "what happened?"

"Could you elaborate?"

"Uh, okay, so we were talking on the phone then Clarence said, 'That can't be good'..."

He shook his head, cutting me off. "No, he said 'That's not good.' Not 'That can't be good,' because 'That's not good' means it's bad, which it was, and 'That can't be good' means there's the possibility it might or might not be bad. There was no might about it. It was bad. Not good."

Clarence bobbed his head in agreement. "He's right."

I bit back the desire to snarl at him, mostly because the nausea was getting worse and any exertion might put my gastric juices over the edge. "Fine. What wasn't good?"

He tipped his head backward and looked to the ceiling in a pensive manner. "We were parked outside of Rick and Rita Ashes's house. It was dark. Pitch black. How you suburbanites manage, I'll never understand. So I was leaning on Clarence's car talking to you about how I'd deciphered Colt's texts, Peggy was standing next to me and Clarence was tip-toeing across their yard. Suddenly, from out of nowhere, that behemoth of a man—Orson, did he say?—appears and lifts Clarence up with his pinky finger."

Clarence snort-laughed. "Huh, yeah, felt that easy." More snorting.

"That would have been, I'm pretty sure, when he said, 'That's not good.'" He leaned to see Peggy. "Would you say?" he asked her.

She nodded. "Mmm mmm."

"In retrospect," he continued, "I shouldn't have disconnected the call, because out of the blue, Rita the man slayer was beside us with a knife shoved into Peggy's ribs." He shook his head as if that might release more information. "She said something to the effect of, 'Follow me and no one gets hurt'. Or maybe it was 'Move and I won't have the Hulk squeeze your friend like a lemon.' Yes, that was it. The Hulk and lemons reference. I remember now."

Peggy nodded some more. "Mmm mmm mm."

"Then Peggy started in on her rambling, which, as we've deduced, resulted in our capture."

"But how did you get here? You couldn't have been in the trunk of her car when she ran me down."

"Nah," said Clarence. "Orson has this boss truck. A real antique. Chevy I think. Ford? Don't know my trucks except this one was old."

Guy added, "They tied us up with duct tape, and the tape roll started running low, but Peggy wouldn't stop talking, so they used what little they had left on her mouth. The ride was miserably bumpy."

He rubbed his bruised cheek with his bound hands and I understood, then, how he'd acquired the black and blue mark.

"Did you scream on the drive here? For help?"

Clarence shrugged. "We tried at first, but," he stopped to scratch his nose with his shoulder. "Why do they always itch when you can't scratch? It wasn't working. The screaming I mean."

"We gave up," agreed Guy.

I snuck a glance at Howard. "How's it going? Any luck?"

He shook his head and stopped chewing for a minute. "How are you feeling?"

I shifted my weight on the floor, going for a more comfortable position, but this only ignited a fiery pain in my ribcage which caused my head to throb harder. But I pasted on a brave face to save Howard the worry. "Fine."

He gave me the same look of doubt I give Callie when she says she doesn't have any homework.

"Really," I said with more conviction. "Not so bad. A teensy bit nauseous, that's it."

"Are you feeling sleepy?"

"A little. What time is it?"

"Don't fall asleep, whatever you do."

Clarence held his bound wrists up for Guy to see his watch. "Two a.m. Well, One forty-nine. Almost two."

"You might have a concussion," Howard said. "Stay awake."

"Honey, I love you and thank you for the advice, but concussion or not, I just don't think I'm going to have trouble staying awake tonight. Not with The Butcher and his two sidekicks, Beauty and the Beast, out there planning our demise. That kind of thing tends to keep me on my toes." I rested my voice for a minute. Talking was more exerting that one would think. "What about you? How did you get here?"

"Easy. Ash had a gun. I have a healthy respect for guns these days. He forced me into his truck and had me drive here."

"I won't say 'I told you so.'" I said.

"That's kind of you," he said with a smile.

The next thing I knew Orson was shuffling back in followed by Rick and Rita. Rick rubbed his beard, Rita played with her hair, and Orson hunched, once again, on the unstable stool.

Rita finally stopped twirling and took a stronger stance with her hands on her hips. "Here's the deal. We're not killers." She threw a leer in Rick's direction. "True enough, there is a dead man in our house, but it was self-defense, I swear." She let out a frustrated sigh and looked to the ceiling. "Do I have to tell them everything?"

"The whole story, as true as it is," drawled Orson.

With another sigh, she continued. "We found this gold-"

"Where'd yoo find that gold? Tell 'em that, Rita."

"On Orson's land. We dug it up on land that we *rented*," she emphasized the word rented and shot Orson a frown. "On land we rented from Orson to grow some very rare and hopefully profitable grapes. The grapes didn't go as expected, but just before the harvest...you get the picture."

"Tell 'em what it is," urged Orson.

She shook her head. "What's it called again, Rick?"

"Munson's Treasure," answered her husband. "Internet articles says it's probably a myth, but it's not looking that way, since it's in the back of my truck right now. Some rich guy by the name of Munson-"

"George William Munson," corrected Orson.

"Whatever," sighed Rick, "George William Munson left to travel North during the Civil War. He left his gold with a farmer."

"He left the gold with Jacob Thaddeus Sparrow, my great, great, great, great grand daddy."

"Sparrow supposedly buried the treasure, Munson never came back for it and when Sparrow went to dig it up years later, it was gone. Or he'd forgotten where he buried it."

"Rick and Rita thought they was goin' to cheat me outta what was rightfully mine, but we come to an understandin' about it, ain't we?"

Howard, for obvious reasons, looked suspicious. "Why are you telling us all of this?"

Rita sighed. She seemed to be tiring of the confession game. "Did you not just hear me? There's a dead man in our basement. Supposedly an expert on historical treasures. Some idiot Rick called, even though I was doing just fine finding the right people, myself."

"Thugs! Your idea of 'the right people' are a pack of thugs." Rick countered. "Koreans, for crying out loud. What do they know about American historical treasures?"

"We care about the money you idiot, not who gives it to us. The bill collectors do not discriminate. And at least I know Kong. You found your guy on the Internet for crying out loud!" Her face was reddening the way mine does when I ask Howard to help around the house and his big contribution is that he washes his own underwear and then wonders why I'm not more grateful.

"Anyway," Rita continued, "this sleaze bucket 'expert' Rick called, showed up at our house two nights ago while Rick was at the bar, and the guy pulled a gun on me. He was going to take the treasure for himself. I wasn't about to let any two-bit, hoze-bag get between me and my money..."

"Whose money?" piped up Orson.

"*Our* money," she corrected herself. "So I kicked him in the balls. He fell backwards and hit his head on an antique claw foot tub that's been there waiting for a remodel."

"He died?" See, I had to ask the question, because she didn't actually say the fall killed him. I like to get my facts straight.

Rita smirked. "You're a smart one, aren't you?"

"So, I don't suppose you had Rick butcher him up and started spreading his body parts out in the woods, did you?"

Both Rita and Rick had matching confused looks on their faces. "Butcher him up?" asked Rita. "The guy's still in our basement, in one piece."

Rick's face did a tilt on that remark. "Well...'in one piece' isn't exactly how I'd put it."

Orson decided to chime in and help us all understand. "He's in the tub soakin' reel good in a warm bath o' Drano," he said.

You could've heard a pin drop.

So, to recap: we had no idea where Colt was, the suburban swingers were only diffident disco-dancers, the *prącia* in the woods didn't belong to

Orson Sparrow, and Rick and Rita Ash just wanted to liquefy an Internet shyster and liquidate some gold.

I tried to process the information and could only come up with one logical conclusion. "Howard," I said, "we are the *worst* investigators ever."

"To be fair," he said, "I'm used to having more technology and reliable data at my disposal."

Yet, the question remained, if we were barking up the wrong tree, why were we now caged like animals?

Guy was probably wondering the same thing. "I suppose dissolving a dead man is one way of going about it," he said. "Yet, I still would have called the police. Because, of course, now you're screwed."

"I know, right?" Rita agreed. "We just keep getting in deeper and deeper. I mean, I couldn't call the police – not after my run-in with the Senator. My credibility was already shot, even though I had an invitation. I had one! The press would slaughter me on this one. A dead guy? Then you bozos show up snooping around. What are we going to do? Kill you all?"

"For the record," interjected Rick. "I voted to keep you alive. But she's the one going to jail, not me."

"I am not going to jail!" she shouted.

"So," I gulped. "You just fed us that whole long sob story about how you're not killers, but now, if I'm reading this right, you've decided you're going to slaughter us anyway?"

She looked apologetic. "Listen, it's not the ideal scene."

My stomach churned like a washing machine set on heavy duty. I sat up and clutched my tummy as best I could with my bound hands. "I think I'm going to be sick."

"She does look a little green," agreed Rick.

"I don't care what y'all say," huffed Orson, "I'm helpin' this little lady." He rose, pulled a pair of scissors out of his back pocket and lumbered my way.

The scissors scared me. Exactly what kind of help did he have in mind? He knelt down and clipped the ribbon around my ankles, and I breathed a sigh of relief.

"Ain't nuthin' more humiliatin' than to yodel your groceries in front o' all the world." Standing above me, he held out a hand. Pleased that his immediate plans didn't seem to involve cutting me to shreds, I reached and he pulled me up gently. Holding down Mama Marr's goulash wasn't easy, but I managed.

"Don't take too long," Rita ordered.

He threw her a disgusted look and led me through the rear door outside, where breathing in the cold night air actually calmed my tummy almost immediately.

Orson motioned to a large plastic bucket with a lid. "Sit down," he whispered. "And lean over if you feel the need."

Leaning sounded like a good idea, so I followed his advice and also took deep cleansing breaths while discreetly patting my jacket pocket to feel for the mace. My heart sank when my hand didn't detect the small spray can. It must have fallen out during my tumble with Rita's car. Not that I had any idea of what I might have done with the weapon, but it would have been comforting to know I had options.

Orson rubbed my back while he continued. "Don't you worry your little head, Mrs. Marr. We're all in one big heap of a mess here, but I think I got us a plan."

"You know who I am?"

"Sure, you're the movie lady. My mama loved the movies too. Why you think she named me Orson?"

"Orson Wells?"

"That's right."

"Are you going to kill us?"

"Now why would I do that?"

"Because...you're the bad guys?"

He shook his head. "I ain't no bad guy, be assured. Got myself into a bit of a pickle just now what with snatchin' you folks against your will, that'd be true enough. That weren't in my original plans, trust me. And Rick 'n Rita, well, they is all kinds of messed up, but they ain't bad to the core. Least wise, I don't think so." He bent closer to look me in the eye. "But there is some bad guys a comin' and I sure would like your help to bring them down. Then we can see about findin' that friend of yours."

CHAPTER SIXTEEN

The large steel door flew open and Rita poked her frowny face out. "Is she done heaving? Time is ticking, time is ticking."

"Why, she's feelin' finer than a frog's hair split four ways and sanded twice," he drawled. "Be back in two shakes of a lamb's tail."

He winked at me and whispered in my ear. "Jest keep an open mind and have a listen to what we have to say. I think this kin work."

Not sure I really had a choice in the matter, I stood when he helped me, and back in we went. Despite their assertions to the contrary, I still clung to the hope that Colt's text code did in fact mean he was somewhere in or around the Ashes's house on Nectarine Drive. I decided the quickest route to the egg had to be through the hen house.

When I reappeared in the doorway of our mini-prison, Howard smiled weakly. "How are you?"

"Didn't yodel my groceries," I quipped. "How about you?"

"We were just having a nice chat. I found out why Mr. Ash is called 'The Butcher.'"

"Oh?" I reached down with my hands, still tied together, and managed to rip the tape off of Peggy's mouth before sitting back down next to her. "There you go, Sweetie."

She yowled for a minute, but was grateful. "Thank you," she whispered, sensing smartly, that she should just keep quiet.

"It's because he is, in fact, a butcher," said Howard.

"*Was* a butcher," Rick corrected. He shrugged. "Long time ago. It paid the bills."

Rita turned her wrist and looked at her watch. "We've postponed this meeting once already, I don't want to do it again. Let's get this plan in action."

"Your plan to eliminate us?" asked Guy. "What a way for a crime reporter to go, huh?"

Orson leaned against the door jam. "Ain't no one gonna liminate no one. Just listen to Miss Rita."

Rita nodded. "Orson says one of you is an FBI agent. Is he right?"

Orson pointed to Howard, "That one's FBI."

Howard rolled his eyes. "Why did you tell him I was a Federal agent?"

"I didn't Howard, I swear."

"Your wife didn't need to tell me nuthin'" said Orson, smiling. "She's that famous lady that writes the movie blogs and gits in all kinds o' trouble. You're famous by dee-fault."

This was a touchy button with Howard and I wasn't happy Orson was pushing it now.

I felt the need to set the record straight. "Technically, he's not with the FBI any longer. He retired."

Poor Rita started twirling her hair again while her eyes moved from a whisker-rubbing Rick to Orson. She didn't seem to be in very good control of the situation.

Orson sighed and stood up straight. "That don't matter none. Miss Rita and Mr. Rick here, have reluctantly arranged for a man they call 'Hammer' to come over tonight and make an exchange of money for the gold. Reluctantly, because this 'Hammer' fella wants more than just the gold. You know who 'Hammer' is Mr. Marr?"

"I do," he answered.

"Please, tell the rest of us," said Guy. "This is beginning to feel like story time at the local library."

"'Hammer' is an anonymous Korean organized crime leader working out of Northern Virginia. They've never been able to get a lead on his true identity," Howard told him. He looked back at Rita. "Let me guess," Howard said, "you met him at Saturday Night Fever? Dr. Kyung Kong?"

"Hooked up is more like it," answered Rick to Howard's comment. "They were having an affair."

Boy, it seemed like there was some swinging going on in the suburbs after all. Rick and Dandi and Rita and Kyung 'Hammer' Kong. As usual, sleepy little Rustic Woods was proving not so sleepy after all. "You mean Kyung Kong is a surgeon and a crime boss?" I asked.

Rita snapped at Rick's accusation. "I told you it didn't mean anything just like your little Southern side-dish didn't mean anything to you." Such a sweet couple. Yeah, they were gonna make it.

Howard turned his attention back to Orson. "What did you mean when you said 'Hammer' wants more than the gold?"

"They is lookin' fer Mr. Rick and Miss Rita to give 'em use of this location fer purposes that are still unclear, but I'm wagerin' they ain't legal if yoo know what I mean." He folded his arms and leaned against the door jam again. "Now Mr. Rick and me, we just want to be able to split our gold three ways and leave here free an' easy. Miss Rita, she's willin' to do what it takes to cinch her spot on that ree-ality show and she figures participatin' in an FBI take-down might just do it fer her." He glanced at Rita. "You were even thinkin' book deal too, right?"

She shrugged. "I'd get my agent on it right away. I mean, if Snooki can get one, why not me?"

Guy got into the conversation. "Have you forgotten that you not only killed a man, but are soaking him in drain cleaner as we speak?"

"It was an accident!" She threw up her arms. "Self-defense. I'm sure a jury will believe me, especially if I help catch some real criminals, right?"

The look on Guy's face was priceless. He gave me a sideways glance that said what I was thinking: *this woman and Snooki have more in common than she realizes.*

"Don't misjudge me by the way I talk, Mr. Marr. I read the newspaper every day and I pay attention to what's goin' on in the world. This 'Hammer' fella is surely on the FBI's radar."

Howard arched his brows, but didn't answer. I knew, however, the cogs of his mind were turning. Finally, he spoke. "What time is this meeting arranged for?"

"4:30 a.m.," answered Rick.

"What time is it now?"

Rick looked at his watch. "2:15."

"That's not enough time to bring in a Federal crew. But I have a better idea that might work if I can get the right person on the phone." He held up his hands, still bound by the plastic bags. "You'll need to cut these if you want my help."

At first, I thought Howard's plan might be to karate chop them the instant his ties were cut, but instead he demanded that all of our bindings be removed, then asked Rick for that phone. It didn't surprise me that the person he chose to call was Eric, although, truthfully, I had no idea what Howard had in mind. I suspected he was playing Rick, Rita, and Orson, but I couldn't be sure. Eric was relieved to finally have heard from Howard—he'd been searching for us since we'd gone missing, and in fact, his next destination was the empty restaurant where we were being held.

After ten minutes of strategizing over the phone, Howard hung up. "He'll call me back in a few minutes, but he thinks we can make this work."

Howard's plan was actually simple. Eric would contact his buddies in the Fairfax police department with the tip that an exchange was about to go down between a restaurant owner and the infamous Korean organized crime boss 'Hammer' who the FBI had yet to locate. The police would jump on it fast, knowing they could take credit for something the FBI had been unable to manage themselves. As a Bureau insider, he knew too well that the FBI loved the spotlight. Consequently, other agencies, bureaus, and departments scrambled like demons when they could prove the Federal attention-seekers less than efficient.

Evidently, I was wrong that Howard was playing our captors. "You mean, you're really going to go after these Koreans?"

"If Eric can pull it together, absolutely." Rick's phone rang in Howard's hand and he answered. A second later he hung up. "They're on the way."

Guy rubbed his hands together with excitement. "An inside story. My luck has changed. My luck has changed."

Rita wanted as much publicity as possible, so Guy was allowed to use the phone to contact his boss who would be asleep, but thrilled to get that kind of call no matter what the hour. Howard knew the Fairfax County police wouldn't be happy about local news crews being anywhere near the area, so he read Guy the riot act and threatened very serious bodily harm if they didn't stay hidden until after police made their move.

"If I wanted to put myself in danger," Guy responded, "I would have chosen to be a war correspondent. Instead, I report on crimes after they happen, and that's how I prefer things. You have no worry, sirs. Hidden we shall remain."

In short time, Eric and a smaller than expected contingent of police arrived, some plain-clothes, some uniformed, and set up the sting operation. Rita and Rick weren't wired in case Kong's men decided to search them. Instead, listening devices were quickly rigged just inside each entrance. Eric was given an ear piece to receive communication from the lead officer on the team, then he climbed into the ceiling and pulled Howard up to join him. Something I was sure wouldn't help his injured leg heal any faster. With help, they were able to mask their presence with the ceiling tiles that had been leaning against the wall.

Because Howard had some familiarity with the Korean language, his assistance was key. Hopefully he'd be able to tell whether the plan was progressing toward the desired end. A hidden video camera was aimed at the door for police to visually monitor the meeting between the Ashes and Kong's crew.

The gold had been locked in the back of Rick's truck this entire time. Orson had Rick give him the keys to his truck so it could be parked in just the right location for them to be able to show Kong the valuable coins, but not allow them access until the agreed upon payment was made.

During the set up, Eric was informed of the dead body melting in the Ashes's basement bathtub, but it was decided, for the safety of the current mission, that no police would be dispatched to their house until after the job was done and the Koreans were in custody. While the possibility was slim that police activity at the Ash house could alert Hammer's crew to a problem, they couldn't risk the chance.

By 4:19, everything was in place and ready for 'Hammer' to arrive. I sat in the back of an inconspicuously parked cruiser, unwilling to leave Howard. Peggy sat with me, willing to wait it out. Guy was in a Channel 10 van with a crew ready to pounce, like the press can do, on the scene the minute an arrest was made. Clarence was invited to join them, and they promised to let him ride along to the Ashes's house afterwards, where Guy would continue his report on the wild shenanigans in the suburbs. Clarence and I were still hanging onto a shred of hope that Colt would be found there.

So basically, I had two jobs to do: sit around and worry. Worrying I could do. Sitting around? Not my strong suit.

CHAPTER SEVENTEEN

The unmarked cruiser we waited in was positioned discreetly at the far, dark end of the very empty parking lot that faced the half-built restaurant. A handy grove of trees that had not been bulldozed during the lot's construction masked us nicely. For the first time that night, I had an outside view of the building where I'd been held hostage. The brick-front structure was larger than it seemed from the inside and if it ever got off the ground, would be an expansive sports bar and grill. But sadly, even though an impressive sign had been raised, it remained unlit. I counted four concrete pads around the perimeter of the huge parking lot—the ground had been laid, but work had been abandoned. It was apparent that this had once been the site for anticipated growth, but I was guessing that the bad turn in the economy had halted the expansion.

With time to kill, I decided to finally ask Peggy why she had been trying so hard to reach me all day.

She made a fist and grimaced. "That Dandi Booker, she screwed me over and I ended up having to pay for all of those goldfish out of my own pocket. They showed me the order with her signature on it." She brushed a lump of stray curls away from her face. "And you know, she isn't so nice as she seems. That's just an act. She tears people to shreds when they turn their backs. People she calls her friends." She was on a roll. "You know Holly Richards, right?"

I nodded.

"She and Holly have lunch at least once a week, sometimes twice. But at the Fall Festival planning meeting, all Dandi did was complain that Holly is so lazy that she has to have a housekeeper and a nanny." She shook her head. "Who cares? I *wish* I had a housekeeper and a nanny. Good on her."

"I'm sorry," I said, patting her hand. "Obviously, Dandi has a few problems of her own." I could have told Peggy about Dandi's drunken fit in the bar, but decided against it. Howard was right, I didn't like the spreading of rumors. Fighting gossip with gossip wasn't the answer. "What about the fish?" I asked. "What did you do?"

She sighed. "I finally found a place that would take them."

"Where?"

"Lake Muir."

Probably my head trauma and lack of sleep accounted for my slow understanding. "What?"

"I dumped every single one of those suckers into Lake Muir tonight. That's where I was before I saw your car. You didn't think I drove that far for milk did you?"

We sat quietly for a minute, then she jumped with excitement. "Oh! And my last call was actually about Roz. She's coming back here for a week."

Now that was exciting news. "Why didn't she call me?"

"She's going to. She needs to ask you if she can stay with you."

"Why is she coming back? She doesn't have family in the area that I know of."

Peggy shook her head. "They haven't received a rent check from your new neighbors in two months and now they're not answering their phone."

When planning their move across country, the first offer Roz and Peter had received on their house fell through at the last minute. They were so desperate that they took the Penobscotts' request to rent with an option to buy after the first year.

I remembered my tree talk with Melody. "That's strange. Melody, the wife, said she got permission from them to take down a tree. So they must have had some conversation."

Peggy shrugged. "That's what Roz said. But it's good for us that we get to see Roz, right?"

"I'll take it."

Peggy smiled and we snuggled close together for warmth and companionship. Nothing like a good friend during a trying time. I vowed never to ignore her calls again.

"I'm sorry," I said after a minute.

"For what?"

"For not believing the best in you."

"None of us is perfect." She squeezed my arm. "But I accept your apology."

A radio squawked in the front seat. "We have movement," a crackly male voice announced. "White delivery truck, unmarked, heading Southwest on Route Two Fifty-four. Should arrive any minute. Do we have video?"

Three of the police cars had visual access to the restaurant and Rick and Rita's activity through wireless video feed. Our car was one of them. "Roger that," our cop responded. "Number two has video."

Another squawk. "Roger, Number three has video."

"Number one is visual," replied another, to make for three confirmed visuals. "Don't move out until I say."

"Roger."

"Roger."

"Roger."

Cop number two, had introduced himself to us as Officer Riker, so I just couldn't resist the urge to make a funny. "Hey, Riker," I said to him, "they got it wrong. You should be Number One. Why didn't you make it so?"

His puzzled expression told me the joke had fallen flat.

"You know." I pressed forward. "*Star Trek the Next Generation?*"

He shook his head.

"I don't get it either," said Peggy.

"Never mind," I said. "It won't be funny now that I have to do all of that explaining. So, Riker, how do we know this is the truck we're waiting for?"

"We don't."

Riker, like most cops I'd met, was small on small talk.

"If it is, and this thing is about to go down, will you be sure to keep my husband safe?"

"Will do, ma'am. Will do." He gave a terse nod. "But from what I heard, that man can take care of himself."

His expression turned serious, his face rock hard. He pulled the radio to his mouth. "I have eyes on the truck. I have eyes on the truck."

Sure enough, from our vantage point, tucked behind some trees on the far end of the parking lot, we could see a large white delivery truck motoring slowly toward the rear of the restaurant. Within seconds, it had moved behind the building and out of our view. Peggy and I scooted forward to see Riker's video display. The image, sent via one of the strategically-placed cameras, showed Rick and Rita pacing in the back hallway waiting to play their part. Rita twirled her hair, then stopped to clench and unclench her hands. She did that a few times, then returned to hair twirling. Rick never stopped rubbing his beard and I wondered if he'd eventually just rub his face clean.

Suddenly, something occurred to me. "Riker? " I asked. "Where's Orson?"

"Who, ma'am?"

"Orson Sparrow. Monstrously huge man, you can't miss him."

He shrugged. "Don't know about that, ma'am."

"Is he in one of the other cars?"

"Nope. Know that for sure. I'm the only one with civilians." He turned and eyed me more directly. "And remember, when I give the word, you two ladies need to get out fast, right?"

We both nodded. That was the only option, since all cars and officers were needed for the take-down, should everything go as planned.

"You sure you'll be okay out here? It's awfully cold."

"We'll be fine," I said.

Back on the video, we saw Rick look toward the ceiling. He seemed to be talking, probably to Eric and Howard, but why couldn't we hear anything?

"Where's the sound?" I asked, starting to panic a little.

Riker tapped his speaker. "Don't know." He got on his radio. "We don't have audio here, over."

"Roger that," someone responded. "Number three dead on audio as well, over. Number one?"

"It appears we have an audio malfunction."

Now I wasn't just a little panicked, I was starting to shake. "That's bad, right? Don't you need audio for this to work?"

"If we want to make an arrest, audio would be good, that's true," said Riker.

He got back on his radio. "Solution, over?"

"We're workin' on it," responded one of the cars. "We're workin' on it."

My pulse raced and I kneaded my hands like balls of dough while Peggy rubbed my back. This couldn't be happening, I thought. Howard didn't need another mission to go badly. Our family couldn't take another wrong turn.

On the video screen, we watched as Rick disappeared from sight then returned just a moment later with a ladder. He pulled something from his pocket, climbed the ladder, lifted the item into the ceiling, descended, and then moved the ladder away.

"What did he just do?" asked Peggy.

I was about to offer my guess when the radio squawked again. "Audio won't resolve. Marr is recording with a cell phone. Male on the floor will signal by cough when the deal is confirmed. Wait for my order to proceed."

Just as Rick returned, his attention swung fast toward the rear door. He threw a look to Rita, waited, shook out his hands in what I assumed was a release of nervous energy, reached for the doorknob, and opened. The two Koreans who had flanked Kyung Kong in Rick's bar earlier that night stood sturdy and erect, with their hands clasped in front of them like a pair of very serious and official-looking identical twins. It looked like some words were being exchanged, then the twin thugs entered and patted both Rick and Rita just as predicted. They then began moving through the restaurant, at which point they were out of view for almost a full minute.

The two suits returned in the shot and opened the door, revealing Kyung 'Thunder' Kong, who proceeded forward. More discussion, from what we could see. The lack of sound made it seem more ominous. My palms sweated so profusely that I was leaving a trail on the back of Riker's vinyl seat.

Finally Kyung signaled to his henchmen, who opened the door. Rick stepped outside, lifted the large bucket that I had used as a seat earlier when sick, and placed it against the door to hold it open. At this point, the camera angle only allowed us a half-view of the back of Rick's truck, placed there smartly by the very-absent Orson. Rick lowered the tailgate and took a step back, allowing the thugs to view inside. It was too dark to see inside the truck bed, so we had to guess they were looking at gold. Kinda wish I could have seen that.

Kong gave a nod, which, roughly translated, probably meant, "looks good to me."

As if on cue, his men stepped to the back of the white delivery truck they'd arrived in, flipped over two locks, and tugged hard on a pull. The door slid up like a shade. Our view of the white truck's interior was far better than that of Rick's truck, mostly because of lighting and proximity. It was still pretty dim, though, and while I clearly could see a huddle of poorly-clothed, disheveled, thin men, the boxes piled high to the ceiling behind them were harder to make out.

"What are those?" asked Peggy.

"I'm guessing cigarettes and slaves," said Riker.

A radio squawked. "This is number one. We have a problem. A man at my window says he wants his wife right now, over."

"Oops." Peggy put a hand to her mouth. "I told Simon I'd be home soon. Sorry!"

I looked at her incredulously. "How did he know you were here?"

"Orson let me call him. He'd been calling hospitals and everything, poor guy."

"But you told him where we were?"

"He promised he wouldn't come."

Riker rolled his eyes and answered the call. "She's here. Tell the husband to stand back and let us do our job."

She pushed open her door. "I'll just get out of your way..."

At that very moment, Rick Ash looked like he made the cough-signal. Riker pointed to me. "Out!"

The radio squawked. "Move in!" shouted Number One.

Peggy slammed her own door as I was opening mine to obey the good officer. But at that precise moment, my eyes caught sight of the video screen.

Howard had fallen from the ceiling.

"Out!" Riker shouted again while my eyes remained frozen on the image.

Peggy had dashed to my side of the car and pulled hard on my arm. "Barb!" she yelled while yanking. I tumbled out and landed on top of her. When sanity took control of my frazzled brain, I rolled over and shoved the door closed with both of my feet. Howard's only hope for a safe return now would be for Riker to get his hiney over there fast. The car peeled out.

"Howard fell, Peggy!" I yelled. "Howard fell out of the ceiling! They'll kill him!"

She grabbed me and hugged me tight. "He'll be okay. I know it."

There we stood, clutching each other, two soccer moms on a glacial, black fall morning in the middle of a deserted parking lot waiting for a major bust that would make the news in just a very short time. I wondered, just for a nano-second, what Dandi Booker would say about that.

The squad cars had sped toward their targets without sirens or flashing lights. Silent seconds turned into minutes while we shivered, wondering if the news was good or bad or ugly. We never heard a gun-shot fired, so that had to be good, we reasoned.

Time kept rolling by unmercifully slow, without word or any sign. Then, just when I thought I might shrivel up from worry and frostbite, more squad cars flew down the road behind us, sirens screaming. A moment later, a dark SUV that I immediately recognized as Simon's rolled up. He motored his window down and flashed Peggy a frown that didn't require a statement for back up.

She was about to open her mouth to explain herself, but was interrupted by the squealing sound of tires spinning and a loud engine revving. Tearing from the other direction at a very dangerous speed, was Rick Ash's pick-up truck. But Rick wasn't driving. Orson was behind the wheel and he had company.

Howard.

I thought I'd faint from relief.

The truck skidded to a stop right next to me and Howard opened the door. "Going my way?"

I waved goodbye to Peggy and hopped in. "Where are we going?"

"Rustic Woods," Howard said. "Rick and Rita Ash's house."

CHAPTER EIGHTEEN

Orson raced Rick's massive pickup so fast I thought the poor thing would collapse like an over-ridden horse. I grasped the dash with one hand and Howard with the other for support, but never asked my new farmer friend to slow down.

It turned out that Orson had never planned on sharing the gold found on his land with anyone. He'd kept Rick's keys after conveniently offering to move the truck, then stowed himself inside the empty dumpster just a few yards away. During the confusion of Howard falling from the ceiling and the mayhem that ensued, he managed to steamroll his way in, lift Howard from the fray, run him to the truck and speed off with the treasure still safe in the back.

The poorly clothed and disheveled men we had spied on the video feed, Howard said, were in very bad condition, but took advantage of the distraction by storming Kong and his men.

"We've seen this before," he said. "It's not pretty. Men and women are promised a better life by men like Kong who bring them here, then turn them into slaves to work off their passage. I wouldn't be surprised if we find out they've been hooked on drugs to control them better." He shook his head. "Makes me sick."

"Then we did a good thing, right?" Orson asked.

"We did a good thing," Howard assured him. "We did a really good thing."

"Officer Riker thought the truck was loaded with cigarettes," I said, still wincing every time we made a fast turn.

Howard nodded. "It's big business. They run them up to New York where the cigarette taxes are so high. Black market cigarettes bring in good money."

I turned to Orson, Colt ever on my mind. "You were in their house? You saw the dead body?"

"That I did." He cringed. "Nasty. Just plain ol' nasty."

"How about Colt?"

He shook his head. "Not a sign of no one else. Sorry. I hope you find him, I really do, but I ain't sure why they'd admit to one dead body, and not up and confess to another."

"Maybe he slipped into the house, searching for something on Rita since he'd been following her, and...I don't know, hurt himself, got locked up somewhere. You know, like when kids accidentally crawl into empty refrigerators..." I knew it was a stretch, but despite Orson's doubts, I believed Colt was there. Everything pointed in that direction. I could tell, though, from his posture and silence that Howard had his doubts now as well.

Soon we were roaring down the toll road. The clock on the truck's dash read 5:29. The sun would be up in a few more hours and Colt would have been missing three days.

Coming off the ramp onto Rustic Woods Parkway, we hit a red light. With not a car in sight on that early Sunday morning, Orson barely tapped his breaks and kept on moving. Two lefts, a right, another ignored red light, another left, two more rights and finally, we reached our destination, but not before Fairfax County Police. The street was ablaze in flashing red, white, and blue lights of police cruisers, fire trucks, and ambulances. A very large forensics van topped off the fleet.

Neighbors stood in robes and slippers on their lawns, some even took pictures with their cell phone cameras. The road had been cordoned off and they weren't going to let us through until Howard saw an officer he knew and explained the situation. That only got us as far as the sidewalk in front of the house however, and because of the Drano mess found inside, no one no how was letting us any nearer. We stood there, helpless, unable to glean any information whatsoever.

Minutes later, a cruiser arrived at the end of the street and Eric flashed a badge. He stopped and talked to two different people before landing by Howard's side. "They're searching the house now," he said. "We should know any minute if they've found Colt."

"They're looking for Colt, right?" I asked. "I mean, they understand a man might be dying in there?"

"Yes, Barb, they do."

Howard pulled me in with his arm and reassured me with his warmth and confidence. "He's okay. This is Colt. We will find him, and he will be okay."

"He's right, Barb," Eric agreed. "Colt will outlive us all." He patted me on the back, then strode across the lawn toward the house.

I tried to believe their words, but my heart was sinking like the Titanic with each passing minute.

Twenty minutes had passed, and now I could see that Guy had arrived with his crew set up outside the barricades. Bright lights on booms illuminated him and his fedora. Off to the side of the crew's work area, was Clarence and Orson leaning against Rick Ash's truck.

Hints of daylight were creeping into the landscape when Eric arrived, a solemn look on his face. Fearing the worst, that Colt had been found lifeless, I started weeping before he could even talk.

"Howard, Barb, he's not there. I'm sorry. There's just no evidence at all that he's been in there." He rested a warm hand on my shoulder. "Now, they did make out some unidentified footprints, probably made by a male shoe, outside near a window in the rear, so I'm trying to talk them into authorizing a canine unit, but they're not very receptive to the idea."

The fact that they'd found no Colt rather than a dead Colt raised my spirits a millimeter or two. I dried my eyes and tried to calm down. "Convince them, Eric, convince them."

"I'm working on it, but I think we need to start looking elsewhere for him. I'm not sure this is the place. I've requested that a team head over to his car and start working up fingerprints and other data. Where is it parked?"

I gave him the address and he disappeared again.

I wondered how Christina Fetty would react to police descending upon the street in front of her house at dawn like this. The dogs would probably go berserk if they were anything like Puddles.

Then it hit me: Frank and Stein. Those dogs had noses just as good as any canine shepherd, I was sure. They sure had the tenacity.

"I need to sit down," I told Howard. "I see Clarence and Orson over there. I'm going to see if I can rest in that truck for a while."

"Have Clarence take you home. I'll let you know how it's going."

"Okay," I said. "Maybe."

Now the thing is, I was pushed to the limit. Not only had I bounced off the hood of a car in motion, but I'd also been off my Slay Menopause diet for a couple of days, so my hormones were probably more erratic than Kim Kardashian's marital status. I'm just setting the stage for the next, very bizarre choice I made, which was not to ask Orson if I could rest in the truck, but instead, to cut through the yards of two complete strangers to Sassafras Street, knock on Christina Fetty's door, and ask her if she wouldn't mind loaning me her dogs to help me find my lost friend, Colt. I never considered she wouldn't be happy to oblige.

As I dashed through the yards, I practiced the wording of my request: "Hi Christina, how are you this morning? Hey, can I borrow Frank and Stein for just a few minutes? I'll bring them back, I promise." I tried to put a less frantic, more logical me in her place and realized that approach probably wasn't the best. I worked another line: "Christina, do your part, save a life, give me your dogs." No, I didn't like that one, either.

I pulled up, panting in front of the Fetty home and saw that Christina was awake. The police had set up camp around Colt's car and one of the officers was questioning her at her door. Christina's brown hair was smooshed to one side as if she'd had a run-in with a failing student at the local beauty school and her pink robe was so bright I'm sure aliens were spotting her from space. She was already having trouble keeping the two mountainous mutts from nosing their way to the policeman's precious cargo. This, I realized, was my perfect chance to help Christina and myself without coming across like Courtney Love on a half-day excursion from the looney bin.

The officer slid me a concerned glance as I stepped past him. "Here, Christina," I said, pushing Frank and Stein back with my whole body. "Let me help you with these dogs. Please, tell this kind officer anything you can remember—he's trying to help us find my friend Colt."

Christina's face shifted from utter bafflement to relieved awareness. She bobbed her head. "Uh huh, uh huh, yup, yup. I see. You haven't found him yet?"

I wanted to slap her silly and scream "What did I just tell you, you silly twit!" but I knew that was just the hormones and possible concussion talking. She was such a nice lady and didn't deserve me even thinking of doing such a thing.

"I'll take Frank and Stein to your backyard for you. Please, continue with the police."

Bobbing her head again, she focused on the uniform in front of her. "Yup, yup, yup," she said. "I'll tell you what I know, uh huh, uh huh."

I wouldn't say that I escorted Frank and Stein to the backyard so much as they hauled me there themselves. With my hands grasped as firmly as possible, one around each leather collar, I guided them to the fence gate at the side of the house. The gate was tall, as it obviously had to be, and the latch was higher than I expected. If I let go of a collar, I might not get the dog back. I'd seen Christina command the dogs to sit before, so I gave it a try and hoped for the best. "Sit!" I whispered to Frank. He only panted, his dish-towel sized tongue hanging out of his mouth. I'm pretty sure he was laughing at me with his eyes. I didn't want to attract unnecessary attention, so I raised my voice only slightly. "Sit!" His obedience wasn't immediate, but eventually, after what I think was a test of my patience, he plopped his bottom down.

"Good," I said. "Stay..." I removed my hand slowly from his collar. "Stay..."

As I reached for the latch, Frank stood and nosed my hand away, while Stein pulled me backwards. Undaunted, I gave it another go. Actually, that's not true. I was daunted. I was daunted big time. My nerves were frazzled, and I was stealing someone's dogs. I still gave it another go, although it was just more of a Lucille Ball go at it rather than a Lara Croft attack of the situation.

"Sit," I said, whimpering now. "Sit, Frank, sit. Do this for me buddy."

He tilted his head in that puzzled way that dogs do. He tilted it first to one side, and then to the other, but he wasn't sitting. Then, without warning, he stood on his hind legs, planted his two bear-like paws on the gate, and began emitting very deep, very loud, very conspicuous barks.

I fell to the ground and began crying again. My jig was up. Any hope I'd ever had of finding Colt was gone. And my ribs were screaming, "Enough! Enough!"

With the sun making its appearance, I sat and bawled while Frank and Stein joined in the chorus.

It wasn't long until I realized Christina was standing above me. "Barb? Are you okay?" She called up to her house. "Howard! She's right here!"

Lovely, kind, sweet, head-bobbing Christina got down on the ground with me and rubbed my back. "Did Frank and Stein hurt you?"

I shook my head. "I was trying to steal them. Do you forgive me?"

Howard was next to me now as well.

"What were you trying to do?" he asked.

"Frank and Stein...sob, sob, good noses...sob, sob, find Colt...sob, sob."

"Barb, we have some news. I don't know if it's good or bad, but we're certain he's not anywhere in the Ash house now."

I brushed my tears away along with some yucky stuff from my nose. "How? Why?"

"Communication here hasn't been the best among the units so not everyone knew the name of the missing person. When they sent a crew over to check out Colt's car, one of them realized what was going on. He told me just now that he gave Colt a ride to our house Friday afternoon because his car wouldn't start."

"He called the police to come get him? Why didn't he call us?"

"He didn't call the police, his cell phone was dead so he started walking to the West Lakes Shopping Center when this cop, a friend of

Colt's, spotted him and stopped to talk. I think the guy said they play poker regularly. Anyway, he gave Colt a ride to our house sometime between four and five p.m. on Friday."

"But that doesn't make sense," I said. "He didn't come to our house."

The world was swirling around me. Every time we opened a door, it lead to another door, but never to an answer. Never to Colt. I started feeling nauseas again. I wiped more tears away and tried to stand, but when I did, the ground went wobbly and my legs gave out. Christina felt my forehead.

"Howard," she said. "She's burning up." She pushed herself from the ground. "I'll be right back. Frank! Stein! Come!"

The dogs followed her into the house and not a minute later, she returned with a puffy floral comforter which she wrapped around me. "Let's get you inside and take your temperature. And I'll fix you a hot cup of tea. Don't worry, I put the monsters in the basement."

She and Howard helped me up. As we walked back to the house, now in good daylight, I noticed that the very back of her yard, some three feet out from the fence, was covered in decorative, white landscaping rock.

White landscaping rock.

Hmm.

"Christina, why the rock?"

She seemed puzzled by my question. "I think she might be hallucinating, Howard. This could be worse than we thought."

"No," he said, understanding my strange query. "She's asking about your landscaping. The white rocks. I'm not sure it's a question, so much as a thought." He was following my drift, I could tell.

Christina's white landscaping rocks reminded me of those in the Penobscotts' yard next door. *Next door*. ND. The *nd* in Colt's text message wasn't code for Nectarine Drive, it was code for *Next Door*.

Maybe we weren't the worst investigators in the world after all. The slowest maybe, but not the worst.

The bobbing commenced. "Yup, yup, yup. Those rocks. Only way to keep the yard from turning into one big mud puddle with the dogs around. Uh, huh, uh huh. Necessity." Then she lowered her voice to a whisper. "Yup, but did you know my neighbor told me, after we put those in, that those kind of rocks are the calling card of," her voice went even lower, just in case the CIA was listening in, "swingers. You know, couples who like to...whoopee, woo-hoo, with other couples." She fanned herself. "Yup, yup, yup, wish I'd known that. I would have chosen river rock!"

"Howard, are you thinking what I'm thinking?"

"It's a stretch," he said, "but you just might be right."

A mask of sheer terror flashed across Christina's face as she apparently misunderstood our exchange. "No, no, no, no, no! I swear, we aren't swingers! We're as normal as white bread and apple pie! I don't even like S-E-X. Ask my husband."

That was more than I needed to know. And evidently more than her husband wanted us to know too, because he was standing on their deck staring down at her, arms crossed, brows deeply furrowed.

Behind him stood Eric, who looked relieved when he saw us. "Thank you," he said patting Mr. Fetty on the back. "Hopefully we'll be out of your way soon." He joined us in the yard. "911 dispatchers took a call from Diane at your house."

"What's wrong? Are the kids okay? What happened?"

"Everyone is fine. She was calling in 'suspicious activity' in your neighborhood. She heard a possible gunshot."

Chapter Nineteen

Aching ribs, fever, and mild hysteria be damned—nothing was going to stop me from getting to my family if they were in danger. Straightening my back, I threw off the comforter and summoned a mother lode of energy and serious intention. "Take me home," I said.

Eric had secured a police cruiser and rushed us home with lights flashing and sirens blaring.

"It's the Penobscotts, Howard," I yelled over the siren shrill. "Colt stumbled into some evil lair of perverted debauchery they're running over there. I knew something was odd about her. People from Wisconsin don't know how to make sushi. A mean Cheddar Mac & Cheese, yes. Not sushi. That should have been my first clue." I know, there I went with the racial profiling again. "Sushi chefs use cleavers, right? Those severed appendages I found in the woods were probably her handiwork. And now she's turned to guns!"

Howard remained more even-keeled. "Your mom could have heard a car backfire and mistook it for a gunshot. Let's stay calm until we know more."

He was right. I worked to calm my nerves, but the constant squall of the sirens made that next to impossible.

"We'll check this out," he continued, rubbing my back, "then I'm taking you straight to the hospital. We should have had you transported hours ago."

When we screeched onto White Willow Lane, two cruisers were already positioned, one in front of our house and one in front of the Penobscotts'. My mother stood in the driveway talking to a uniformed

145

policeman while another could be seen knocking on the front door of our neighbor's house. I flew out of the car and up the driveway as quickly as my battered legs would carry me.

"Please do not question my hearing, young man," she scolded him. "That is blatant age-ism. A recent visit to the doctor revealed that these ears work just as well as those of any twenty-year-old. I most definitely heard two powerful gunshots that rocked the foundations of my daughter's house." When she caught sight of me, her frown deepened. "Barbara, you look terrible."

I coughed. "That's funny, because I'm sure I feel way worse than I look."

Eric flashed his badge and the censured cop sighed in relief. "When did you hear the shots, Diane?" Eric asked her.

Seeming appeased, she rattled on, but didn't exactly answer the question. "Thank goodness you're here now, Eric. Possibly you can teach this rookie a thing or two. For instance, to believe a rational woman when she reports the discharge of a weapon. I told him I was a graduate of the County Citizen's Police Academy. I know whereof I speak."

The "rookie's" radio squawked. "Not getting an answer here," came a static-laced report, from what I assumed was the officer investigating next door. A quick look-see confirmed he was on his radio. "Checking the rear of the premises," he added.

"Roger that," answered his colleague, who appeared desperate to leave his current station and join him.

Eric offered him the out he was looking for. "I've got it here," he said. "Give him backup."

The grateful policeman nodded and literally dashed away. That's my mom. She even scares uniformed lawmen packing heat.

Howard caught a glimpse of something and tipped his head toward our house. "Barb, we have spectators."

I looked up to see several eyeballs peering through the upstairs window in Callie's room. Mama Marr and the three girls had collected there to view the exciting goings-on.

"We should go let them know we're okay," I said.

With a nod, he joined me on the brick path that lead to the front door. "You're not exactly okay," he said.

"I'll put on a good show."

As we approached the house, he called back. "Fill us in when you know anything, Lamon."

Still Brad-Pitt handsome despite his desperate lack of sleep, he gave a nod. "Will do." Then he turned back to sweet-talk my mother. "Now, Diane," he said, all smiles, "tell me when you heard the shots."

We'd barely reached our front step when she interrupted her own description of the gunshots to point out activity at the Penobscott house. "My. Someone has finally decided to answer the door," she said.

Howard and I turned at the same time to catch sight of Neil Penobscott not just "answering his door," but blasting through it and out onto the front lawn, his arms raised high in the air, screaming, "Don't shoot! Don't shoot! My wife's gone crazy! She's got a gun and a hostage! Don't shoot!" He fell to his knees on the frost-glazed grass.

Eric was on the move when the early morning air was filled with the bold and unmistakable blast of heavy weaponry. Even my mother yowled at the crack which rang from inside the Penobscotts' house.

Howard threw the door open and shoved me in. "Upstairs and stay there!" he shouted. He pointed a stern finger in my face. "Stay there!" My mother was on his heels, not messing around. She might have had a diploma from the Citizen's Police Academy, but she also apparently wanted to graduate on to another year of life on earth. She sped around him, through the door and upstairs faster than the Road Runner looking for a pile of Acme bird seed.

But I could see Howard had no plans to join us. He tried to close the door behind her, but I threw my foot in the way. "Howard, you're unarmed, you can't!" I grabbed his wrist and pulled hard, straining my own ribs. "Get in here!"

"I won't put myself in danger, I promise."

How could he promise such a thing? He was crazy. "Lock the door," he said, escaping my grasp, and running away, not a hint of a limp in his gait.

At his core, Howard was a hero, a man who believed in facing any dangerous scenario head-on to protect others. I knew he had no choice in his own mind. I locked the door, genuflected even though I wasn't Catholic, asked Buddha to send a dose of good Karma our way, and followed my mother up the stairs to Callie's room.

Amber and Bethany gravitated to my side like magnets. I'm not sure I could have peeled them away they were stuck so tight. Mama Marr was beside herself with fear for Howard.

"My son, what is he doing? He doesn't have the guns or no thing and there is the shooting!" She pointed to the Penobscotts' house. "This is worse than Philadelphia, this Rustic Woods." She shook her head while my own mother tried to comfort her with little pats to the back.

"He'll be just fine, Alka. Your son is one of the strongest, smartest, bravest men I know. I'm proud to have him for a son-in-law."

I was far too terrified to ruminate long on her accolades or their contradiction to the many less celebratory opinions she'd expressed about Howard over the years, but the praise was duly noted.

Callie's room sits in the upper corner of the house facing the street. It has two windows, one looking out onto White Willow Lane which also gives her a nice view of the Penobscotts' front yard. The other window, on the side of our own house, faces the side of the Penobscotts' property, their back yard, and the woods behind. From our vantage point, staring out of the front-facing window, we could see Officer Lamon inside the police cruiser at the end of our driveway and Howard, kneeling on the road beside him, using the driver's side door open to protect him from God knew what. Lamon was on the car radio, probably calling in the troops. The door-knocking cop had made it back to the same car, hiding behind the passenger's-side door, while it appeared that Neil had been directed to the back seat.

Realizing that the girls should not see Howard in danger, especially Callie, who didn't need to witness a repeat of our August trauma, I told them to move to Amber's room and close the shades.

"No!" they screamed in unison. "We don't want to be alone!"

"You won't be alone," my mother cooed in an unusually soothing tone. She really could be warm and consoling when she wanted to,

I thought. I imagined her with those babies in the hospital. "I'll go with you." She opened her arms wide and scooted them out the door. "Alka, would you like to come?" she asked.

Mama Marr was adamant, her head shaking firmly. "No. I stay." Her fingers gripped the window sill in case anyone should try to remove her with force. "I stay," she repeated.

Unable to locate the young policeman who'd been reprimanded by my mother, I slipped over to the other window for a better view of the Penobscotts' side and back yards. There, I spotted him creeping slowly around the corner of the house. Another shot rang out and he fell to the ground. By the way he dropped, I just knew he had taken a bullet rather than a dive for safety.

Then I spotted movement in the far corner of their property, right at the tree line.

The jeans and the blond hair were unmistakable.

Slithering on his stomach into the woods like a snake, was Colt.

Colt was alive.

CHAPTER TWENTY

I screamed out the window to Howard, who was still in the cul-de-sac, ducked behind the police cruiser. "Howard! Colt! Backyard," but he didn't turn his head. "Howard!" I screamed again. "Anyone! Help him!" Nothing. We were too far away, the commotion in the street was too loud, and my voice just floated away on the cool, fall breeze.

Something had to be done. Crazy-wife-with-a-gun, Melody Penobscott, was out there shooting people left and right. Colt was being hunted down like sick prey and no one knew. I tore out the room and took the stairs three and four at a time, stumbling on the last step and splaying face down onto the foyer floor. Bump in the road. I ignored the shooting pain in my side and scrambled up. Mama Marr hollered after me, "What you do? Where you go?"

"Mama, get to Howard! Tell him it's Colt! He's heading for the woods!" I shouted back.

We don't keep guns in the house, I won't allow it. FBI agent or no, I absolutely cannot tolerate a firearm in my house with children around. I will admit, at that very moment, I regretted my hard stance on the subject. A loaded gun would have been handy. Never fear, though, I had a kitchen full of killing machines. Or at least a steak knife or two.

Rifling through my drawers, I also began to regret my poor attention to all things culinary. I was a 46 year-old married woman and mother of three, and yet I did not even have a proper set of knives. We had one chopping knife—if that was what it was called—who knew? I chopped with the thing. Sometimes. But it was easily twenty years old

150

and the tip was broken off. That wouldn't work. There were the steak knives, somehow those didn't seem quite menacing enough. Time was running out if I wanted any chance of intercepting Melody and saving Colt's life, so I grabbed the scariest thing in my messy utensil drawer: my pasta spoon.

Keep reading. It's scarier than you'd think.

I flew out the back sliding glass door. My backyard met seamlessly with the Penobscotts', since neither yard was fenced, and both were bordered by the same woods I had walked the previous days. I slipped into the woods with one goal: rescue Colt. Did I want to be a hero? Heck no. Did I see a choice? Not really. If I had run out into the cul-de-sac to warn the tiny brigade of three, precious time would have been lost and Colt could have been dead. The best case scenario had me locating Colt and bringing him to safety without ever encountering Melody or her firearm. The worst case scenario...was worse.

The ground beneath my feet was buried in damp leaves and golf-ball sized acorns, so I kept slipping and losing my balance while I tried to maneuver between the trees and lock my radar onto Colt's where-abouts. It was one thing to see him from a second story window, but down on the ground, my bearings were twisted. I wondered if Mama Marr had made it to Howard yet. Backup with matching fire-power was a far better prospect than going it alone. My pasta spoon would be very intimidating, I knew, but I wasn't naive enough to believe it could stand up to the threat of a loaded barrel in my face.

A whisper caught my attention. The voice was Melody's. "Colt? Where are ya? Come on out. I won't hurt ya."

For a selfish moment, I wondered why the cuckoos always latched on to me. Then I realized this one had latched onto Colt and I was just along for the ride. That nutcase would rue the day she messed with Colt Baron and his friend, Barbara Marr.

Melody didn't sound inches away, but she didn't sound very far either. I knelt low to the ground behind a fat oak tree, scanning for both of them, glad for once, that my old jacket was so faded—hope-fully it offered me some camouflage. Leaves rustled, but I couldn't tell from where. My heart pumped so furiously that my breathing became hard to control. I couldn't let her hear me. As I covered my mouth to muffle the sound, I noticed my breath in the air and realized I should be looking for evidence of their respiration, not just their bodies.

Melody whisper-shouted again. "Hey baby, don't you know I love you?"

As soon as I heard her voice again, my eyes watched the air nearby. Bingo. From behind a tree far to my right, I saw the condensation of her breath as the words spilled out. Still though, Colt was at large.

"Colty..." she continued with more edge in her voice. "The police are after us and you're starting to-"

As I moved one leg to get a better footing, a twig snapped under my foot, interrupting Melody's psycho-attempt at wooing. She moved from behind the tree and began treading in my direction.

"Colty? Is that you? This is getting serious." The deranged and irritable tone in her voice rose sharply.

I had to admit, I was becoming irritable as well, unable to locate Colt and wondering where Howard and those police were with their weapons. Knowing I had to get out of Melody's way fast, I planted myself stomach down on the ground and began wiggling backwards toward the steep slope that led away from the houses and down to the path. Something sent Melody moving in the opposite direction, so I struggled to get on my hands and knees to better look for Colt, only gravity kept pulling me down the slope. I reached for a twiggy baby tree with my left hand, straining with all of my might and had just managed to brush it with my fingertips when something cold and wet landed on my pasta spoon hand. My scream was instinctual and, unfortunately, I couldn't take it back.

Melody was heading my way again, faster now, louder, with more confidence.

"Curly," croaked a voice.

The something that had grabbed my hand was Colt. As I furiously brushed leaves away from the lump next to me, more and more of him appeared. He was pale, drained, and dirt-covered, but he was alive. He must have crawled to the spot and covered himself with leaves to hide from Melody.

"You found me," he whispered.

I smiled and gave a nod.

He coughed quietly. "Took you long enough."

"She's coming this way," I whispered in his ear. "Can you move?"

"Pretty...sure." His breath was raspy.

I peered behind us, down the long, steep slope. Finally, the sound of approaching sirens told me more help was on the way. The police could be just seconds from finding Melody and thwarting her, but I couldn't take any chances. I certainly couldn't scream to gain their attention, or she might shoot. If, however, Colt and I were able to make our way safely to the walking path, a bridge lay just around a bend. I remembered that it was still well-covered on both sides by heavy brush and a shallow creek ran underneath. I'd move us in that direction thinking it could provide us necessary concealment.

"Slide backwards, hang on to me."

He didn't say anything, but weakly raised his thumb to indicate he was on board. Down we slid, over leaves and sticker vines and fallen branches both large and small. The ride was filled with bumps and jolts that irritated the burn in my ribcage. Colt grunted the whole way down, so I suspected he was in a great deal of pain as well. Once we reached level ground near the path, I prayed a jogger bearing a concealed weapon for safety would appear, but such was not our luck. Rest would have been nice, but there was no time. A quick peek up the hill told me Melody was hot on our trail.

"Can you walk?" I whispered.

He winced. "My ankle." His voice had gained a hint of strength.

"Which one?"

He patted his right leg.

I pointed down the path. "Lean on me, we're going that way."

Together we struggled, lifting here, pushing there, pulling arms around, until I had as good a grip on him as possible and we could begin hobbling with great effort toward the bridge. I stayed just off the path in the brush to camouflage our images from Melody. Colt bit his lip hard with each step.

I wondered why the police hadn't come to our rescue yet. And where was Howard? Certainly Mama Marr had delivered my message by now.

Every couple of steps I looked back, hoping for signs of Melody or—better yet—rescuers. Neither were in sight, and as we drew closer to the bridge, I began to have hope that Melody might have finally been apprehended.

"Colt," I said quietly. "We're almost there."

"Where is she?" he moaned.

"I don't hear or see her. Maybe she's caught."

Voices rang in the distance. Men's voices, hollering. Help was on the way. I sighed in relief and we turned instinctively toward the sound of our saviors.

"Hey! We're here! Down here!" I yelled.

"So, you are," said a voice rising from the shallow stream bed. Melody had snookered us. She might have been a fruitcake, but she was a crafty fruitcake. The way she'd gotten down to that creek bed without being spotted was just too creepy. We began inching sideways toward the bridge as she climbed up the gentle embankment, the gun dangled from her hand that hung at her side. A long abrasion on the right left side of her face oozed blood. Her bouncy pony-tail, I noted, remained intact. "Hey, Barb, whatcha doin' with my man?" she asked, once on flatter ground, the gun still dangling.

"In case you didn't notice," grunted Colt, "she has issues."

Melody sneered.

With the deadly firearm in her possession temporarily off duty, I decided now was the time to bring out the pasta spoon and catch her off guard. See, the pasta spoon had been broken for years. The spoon part of it kept coming off the metal spiked arm, and we had discovered long ago that, if whipped just right, the thing could fling off clear across the room and possibly put an eye out. I was praying now would be one of those times. "Melody," I said, readying the utensil, "he's not my man..." I raised that pasta spoon high in the air, bit back the urge to scream from the resulting pain in my side, and flicked the kitchen utensil hard like a whip. As it always did, the spoon portion sailed through the air. "And he's not yours either!"

Before the word 'either' was out of my mouth, the pronged end had already buzzed past her head, missing her and both of her eyes by several inches. I regretted not choosing the steak knife.

Colt was kind in his assessment. "Nice try, anyway."

Melody laughed, which I didn't begrudge her, since it was a laughable move, then raised her gun.

"Barb, if you don't give him to me, I'll make sure he'll never be anybody's man."

Colt and I started inching around, back toward the bridge. He was heavier than me, and I was finally beginning to buckle under his weight, afraid I might collapse altogether.

The hollering voices had gotten louder, but there was still no one in sight.

Melody, seeming aware that pursuers were closing in, aimed her gun square at Colt's chest. "Why don't you love me the way I love you? It could have been so wonderful. But now you've gone and made it, just like all of the rest."

She swiveled the gun toward me. "And you. You don't deserve him."

By now, Colt and I were backing our way onto the bridge and Melody was on the path. Her eyes were wild like a caged animal, but they never strayed. She was focused on us entirely.

I wanted to shout out, giving the police a beacon to locate us, but the risk was too great.

Finally, I heard the sweet sound of crunching leaves. Several figures were making their way toward us from the left. Howard was the first to arrive slowly and cautiously, followed by Eric and another uniformed man. They maintained a safe distance, but Eric and the cop raised their guns on Melody.

"Put the weapon down," Eric said. "Melody, lower it slowly to the ground."

She didn't bat an eye, didn't flinch a muscle. Her gun just kept jumping from target to target. She was going to shoot one of us, it was just a matter of which one.

155

"Men," Howard said slowly, calmly. "Stay back. Don't shoot."

"That's right, men," she answered, staring us down. "Don't shoot, because if you do, I'm not going down alone. I'll take one of them with me. Will it be," she aimed the gun at my head. "Her?" then at Colt. "Or will it be the womanizer?"

I'd been so busy dividing my attention between Melody's gun and Howard and his crew that I hadn't noticed that my mother, of all people, had somehow made her way to the path. She ran toward us now and honestly, the only thing that went through my mind was, "What the hell?"

For a very large and aging lady, she managed to sprint as quietly as a mouse. Melody never heard her coming. "You want to shoot someone you slimy, weak-minded, runt?" she said, stopping and planting a firm High-Noon, western sheriff's stance. "You shoot me."

"Weak-minded?" shouted Melody. She swung around, full of fury, searching to aim at the woman who challenged her.

And if my mother's appearance wasn't enough of a surprise, what happened next was even more shocking, and certainly deserving of a title in the record books.

As soon as Melody had turned to face my mom, an iron skillet whizzed past from the side of the bridge, flying high through the air, spiraling handle over pan over handle, and finally landing squarely in the middle of Melody Penobscott's back.

She fell in a heap on the ground.

"That's what you get," said my mother, "for trying to hurt my daughter."

When I turned to see who had wielded the killer skillet, I saw Mama Marr grab the bridge for support. A wide smile graced her chubby face and she raised her fist in the air like a miniature Rocky. "That'll show her never to mess with no skillet-throwing champion. We got her good, eh, Diane? We make the good team!"

Mama Marr proved she was far better with an iron skillet than I was with a wonky pasta spoon.

CHAPTER TWENTY-ONE

Mama Marr saved the day, but her frying pan only maimed Melody Penobscott. Emergency responders rushed the psycho killer to Fairfax General under police escort while Colt and I were transported to Rustic Woods Hospital just around the corner. Howard wanted to ride with me in the ambulance, but I insisted he stay with the girls to keep them calm and let them know everything would be just fine. He held my hand and rubbed it gently while the EMTs positioned Colt.

"Hey," I asked him. "You think they offer a frequent customer discount at the hospital?"

He smiled.

"You know—three visits to the ER, get the next one free? They should consider it."

"You sure I shouldn't come with you?"

I shook my head adamantly. "No. The girls need you right now. I have, what? A cracked rib, maybe, and a fever. They'll release me in a few hours, but the girls will be worried sick." I pointed my head toward a huddle of policemen interrogating my mother and his. "And it looks like Cagney and Lacey there will be tied up for a while."

His sexy, droopy Italian eyes were even droopier from strain and the lack of sleep. He ran grimy fingers through his dark-but-graying hair and rolled his eyes at my comment. "What is it with the women in this family?"

"We get things done."

"I can't argue with that."

Three paramedics descended upon me and my gurney. One addressed Howard. "We need to ready her for transport, sir."

He nodded and kissed my hand. "Be with you soon."

I frowned slightly. "Anything you'd like to add to that?" They were hoisting me into the ambulance, opposite Colt.

He smiled again. "I love you?"

"Are you asking me or telling me?"

"I love you."

"That's better. I love you too."

He waved, and soon he was out of my sight.

"Always the happy lovebirds," Colt slurred as I was jostled into place. "You lucky dogs. Me, I get the lady from Misery."

"How are you feeling?"

His lips curled barely, his eyes lids fluttered. "Feeling nothing now that Mr. Blue is here."

For a minute I thought he was hallucinating until one of the medical technicians saw my confusion and explained. "We gave him morphine for the pain." A slight jolt was followed by the wail of a siren.

"You wanna hear my sad story?" Colt asked on route.

"If you feel up for it."

"You know me," he said, a thin smile on his lips, "I'm always up for anything."

The trip to Rustic Woods Hospital was fast, but Colt relayed a good portion of his story with surprising coherence.

Colt had been having one of those days. First his cell phone died while tailing Rita Ash, then his car wouldn't start. "My buddy, Chunks, gave me a ride to your place."

"Chunks?"

"Nickname. Long story involving alcohol and pizza rolls."

That was a story I didn't need to hear. "He's a cop, right?"

He nodded. Colt went on to explain that just after he was dropped off at the end of our driveway, Melody Penobscott, who he'd just bequeathed the new nickname, "Maniacal," jumped on him like a honey bee to a sunflower. "She asked me to help her unscrew a bolt from a chair she was refinishing. I said, 'sure' 'cuz that's just the kind of guy I am. Help a damsel in distress and all that...you know...manly stuff."

"You're very manly," I agreed.

"Tell me something I don't know. Anyway, she repaid me with a conk to the head instead of a simple 'Thank you.'"

He licked his lips, waited a beat, then recounted the events after regaining consciousness from her attack. He came to on a mattress in a cramped dark room with his right hand handcuffed to a pipe above his head. A tiny reading lamp had been placed on a table with a small glass of water. From the tight and musty confines, he deduced that he was being held captive in a crawlspace under the house.

Melody had found his cell phone but must have determined it was dead since she left it on the ground. It was barely out of his reach, but not entirely. He was able drag it with a foot and charge the battery by placing it under his armpit for the heat, just the way Guy had deduced. The charge was enough to get short messages out, but not enough to make calls. Each time, he'd have to recharge. After the last text, she caught him putting the phone back in place so she punished him by taking away the water and light.

Colt decided the only way to escape was to play into her fantasy and woo her. He was eventually able to convince her to lay down with him. When she fell asleep, he slowly wiggled a single bobby pin out of her hair and waited. When she woke up she decided he deserved a big homemade breakfast for being such a loving hostage. She was just covering the entrance to the crawlspace with a bookshelf when Colt heard a man's voice.

Hoping it was help on the way, Colt hollered while unlocking his handcuff with the bobby pin. Once his hand was free he pushed on the back of the bookshelf that separated him from freedom. Hollering and pushing, he eventually toppled the shelf and crawled out into the dank basement. Not seeing a door out, he tore up the stairs and through a door onto the Penobscotts' main floor where he found Melody aiming a gun at her own husband.

Colt was thinking of making a run for it until Melody shot two holes in the floor to show how seriously demented she was. I figured those must have been the shots my mother heard. A crazed Melody ordered them both into the basement while she "decided what to do next."

I did a quick mental calculation. "It had to have been at least ten minutes, maybe more, between those first two shots that my mom heard, and the second one we heard. What was she doing all that time?"

"Sewing a dress for the lunatics' prom maybe. Who knows?" His eyes started to droop. "We heard a lot of stomping and door banging until the doorbell rang."

"That's when you made your escape?"

"Not right away, but that's...the general idea." The morphine was really kicking in and he was fading fast. "We were supposed to divide and conquer. Things went a little screwy, as you can see. That chick is strong for being so skinny—lifted a steel statue from her mantle like it was a piece of paper." His eyes drooped more while he paused. "Didn't feel like paper when it landed on my ankle."

"You're safe now at least."

"I'm not the first." Colt coughed and closed his eyes. "There was blood on that mattress, and it wasn't mine."

I didn't bother to tell Colt, just then, about the body parts Puddles and I had found in the woods. But it didn't take a rocket surgeon to figure out where they'd come from or that Melody liked to chop more than fish for making sushi.

As Colt was hoisted from the ambulance, it occurred to me that dream-Frankie's advice not to show the pain probably saved Colt's life. If I had gone to the hospital earlier, I wouldn't have been there to rescue him from the deadly grip of Maniacal Melody Penobscott. Thank goodness for wacky hallucinations.

⚜ ⚜ ⚜

As it turned out, my visit to the hospital was longer than just a few hours. Just waiting for x-rays seemed to take half the day. A dose of acetaminophen and a fluid drip brought my fever right down. My rib-cage would be bandaged for support to heal the one broken rib I'd incurred. Howard came over with the girls who were allowed to sit with me while he checked in on Colt and a very relieved Clarence. When he returned, he gave me Colt's medical update: his right ankle was in bad shape and his left tibia had sustained a hairline fracture. His doctor was amazed that he even managed to put any weight on the left leg at all without crumbling in agony. The ankle was repairable with surgery and they would have to set the left leg. He'd have to remain off his feet for several weeks.

"What is it with the men in my life?" I asked him, grinning when Howard returned with the news.

"We get things done, too." He shrugged. "We just break a few bones in the process. Colt's worried about being out of work."

"I know. If he doesn't work, he doesn't earn money."

Howard nodded and although he didn't say anything, I knew the wheels of his mind were turning.

"What are you thinking?" I asked.

He rubbed a finger along my arm. "The best thing would be if someone could help him out. With the business. You know, while he's recovering."

"Who would this someone be? You? Playing private detective?"

"I have the time. He was there for me—us—when we needed him. Now I can return the favor."

The wife part of me that loved to see my husband healthy and in one piece did not like the idea. Not one bit. The wife part of me that loved to see my husband happy and productive, doing what he did best, knew it was the way things had to be.

Howard's phone jingled. He answered and the following conversation seemed largely one-sided. Howard said, "Uh huh" and, "You don't say," a few times, but that was about it. He finally ended with "Thanks for keeping me in the loop, Lamon. Let me know what else you learn," and clicked his phone off. He pulled some dollar bills from his wallet and sent the girls to go get snacks from the vending machines in the waiting room.

When they had left, he let out a sigh of disbelief. "That was Eric."

"I got that. What did he say?"

"Remember that noise we heard the other night?"

I cringed. "Chain saw?"

He gave a slight nod. "Chain saw." He ran his hands through his hair. "Those items you and Puddles found in the woods on Friday belonged to the man she was...disposing of. That joke I made about her killing someone and feeding the body in bits and pieces to the foxes—that's exactly what she was doing. Eric said she used a variety of tools to do her work."

My stomach turned at the thought. "Let me guess: one of those tools was a cleaver?"

"Cleaver. They don't know the identity of the victim, but evidence in their home is suggesting she's had some connection to that swingers' club in Ashburn Heights. The husband...I forget his name..."

"Neil."

"Right. He had no idea. He met her less than a year ago. She's wanted for two similar murders in North Dakota. One of them, her husband before this one."

I took a few more deep breaths. "Colt could have been next."

"He wasn't."

"Or you. You're handsome. You're sexy. You're-"

He interrupted my panic attack with a soft, warm kiss that lingered. "You're pretty sexy too."

"Really? Now you get passionate? When I'm in a hospital about to be wrapped like a mummy? Your timing is way off, Mister." Of course, I was teasing. Truthfully, I was excited to feel Howard's heat again. Although, his timing *was* off a little. We'd have to wait for that rib to heal.

CHAPTER TWENTY-TWO

A week later found big changes brewing in the Marr household. We moved Mama Marr in with my mother, since they really did make "the good team." The move also reunited her with Pavrotti, which caused her great happiness. Colt moved in with us temporarily while he recovered. We had to turn the living room into a makeshift bedroom, which didn't give anyone a whole lot of privacy, but sometimes you gotta do what you gotta do. Everyone pitched in to wait on him when needed, but a recent frequent visitor, Shin Lee, had started helping out as well. Seemed she and Colt had some mutual attraction simmering between them, and if things continued, I imagined they'd progress to a roiling boil once he was mobile again. Truthfully, I wasn't thrilled he was romancing a married woman, but she had filed for divorce, so who was I to offer an opinion? He was a grown man who'd been through enough, and she seemed to make him happy. I kept my mouth shut.

The bust that took down Shin's criminal husband, Kyung 'Hammer' Kong, proved very fruitful for Fairfax County Police since they were able to glean long-sought information from the men kept as slaves. Each day, the news reported increasingly frequent arrests throughout the county. It seemed the men locked in the back of that moving truck were only the tip of a monstrously huge human trafficking iceberg within the Korean community. Howard said the problem was well known in the law enforcement world, but not among the general population. While the press will jump on the smallest drunken escapade of the latest teen celebrity heartthrob, news of men and women being confined like cattle and forced into cruel labor, prostitution, and involuntary organ donation doesn't bring in the ratings, so falls to short blips of internet interest. I vowed to sit down with Guy Mertz once I felt better and see what we could do about that.

On the Orson Sparrow front, he dodged the dicey issue of kidnapping. Had the Korean syndicate raids not gone so well, he might have faced charges, but given the success of his enterprising plan, Orson was spared any arrest or legal action. Even better, he kept his gold along with an amazing discovery: an official will found buried underneath the treasure, written by George William Munson, giving Jacob Thaddeus Sparrow one half of his land upon his death. Obviously thrilled, Orson was working through the proper channels to see what, if anything, could be done about that. At the very least, he was in possession of a prized piece of historical interest. He had already been interviewed by Channel 10 and would soon be making an appearance on The Today Show.

Rick and Rita Ash got nothing, zip, zilch, nada. Well, I take that back. They got none of the gold since Orson had been so sly, but they both got jail time. Seems the authorities didn't care a hoot that they'd assisted in the arrest of Kyung Kong, but they did care a whole lot about the dead guy stewing in Drano soup. Rita, though, blissfully believed that the publicity would still land her that Happy Housewives gig and a seven-figure book deal. According to Eric, that hadn't happened yet.

And me? I was doing well. The impact with Rita Ash's Mercedes did, in fact, crack a lower rib on my right side, but the damage was minimal and already I could take a deep breath without wanting to shriek in pain. And on Saturday, just a week after Howard and I started searching for Colt, I was sitting in an art studio with my mother and Mama Marr, trying hard as I might to produce something better than a gangly stick figure. I mean, the ladies saved my life, was I really going to bail after that? And, to be honest, I didn't really mind. I'd developed a deeper appreciation for my own mother, who'd proved she would lay down her own life for her child just as I knew I would for mine. Possibly—okay, probably—as with my friends, I also often thought the worst of my mother rather than the best.

"Barbara," my mother said, peering at my sorry rendition of the naked male figure standing before us. "Do you think you have his—"

"Don't say it, Mom." My muscles tensed while I actively reminded myself that she had risked her own life for mine.

"Say, '*prqcia*' Diane," Mama Marr whispered. "She likes the word better."

My mother grimaced and pushed her glasses up higher on her nose. "I wasn't talking about his '*prqcia*,' I wondered why she has his arm in such an odd location. See," she pointed to the male model in the center of the room. "His arm," she tilted her head. "Both of them actually, are up higher."

An artist, I am not. See, that wasn't his arm I was drawing. Mama Marr was correct.

I bit my lip and just kept drawing, because really, it wasn't about improving my sketching skills so much as spending time with the women who would both rescue me from the deadly aim of a flipped-out fruitcake, and yet frustrate me greatly all at the same time. I guess that's what family is all about. You take the good with the bad.

Oh, and I agreed to start volunteering at the hospital in the pediatric ICU ward once my rib had healed. I'd probably never be able to appropriately represent a *prqcia* on paper, but I knew I could offer a "baby in need" some tender loving care. That didn't require talent, just heart.

And speaking of love...

CHAPTER TWENTY-THREE

As the days grew colder and Thanksgiving decorations were re-placed with Christmas trees and pine scented candles, Colt and I both healed nicely while Howard took the reins of Colt Baron Private Investigations. In fact, he did so well and brought in so much money in that short amount of time that they decided to change the name: Baron and Marr, Investigations Unlimited. Howard had a continual smile on his face and a little jump in his step and no limp at all. The man was back on his game.

Howard and I both, like many dieters, decided to put the Dr. Sadistic food restriction plan on hold until after the New Year, but to assuage our guilt, we adhered to the daily supplement regimen with nearly religious fervor. And I will say, I think that bald spot was beginning to fill in again.

One Saturday night, Howard surprised me in the kitchen while I was trying to decide what to fix for dinner. "You know that blue dress I love so much?"

Did I know? That was my "lucky" dress, if you know what I mean. "Yes..." I answered playfully, closing the refrigerator door. "I think I remember the one."

"Why don't you go put it on."

"I don't like to cook in my dressy clothes, honey. They get all messy. Who likes messy dressy clothes?"

"Maybe I have plans that don't include cooking."

Colt and Shin had been in the living room watching TV and Colt couldn't resist the urge to chime in. "Sounds like there's some sort of cooking in the plans!" he yelled.

"Keep your nose in your own business, Mister," I responded, while throwing Howard my super sex-me smile. "Or I'll tell Shin to take you back to her place."

I heard Shin commenting that my idea wasn't such a bad one at that.

"So," I continued, pulling Howard closer. "What are your plans?"

An hour later, with me in my blue dress and Howard in a dapper gray suit and tie, a fancily clad waiter was pushing in my chair for me and draping a cloth napkin in my lap. Howard, it seemed, was romancing me in a very posh and very charming Italian restaurant on the shore of Lake Muir. He was being positively chivalrous. And yes, I was eating it up. We sat in a dark corner, sipped a fine red wine, held hands across the table, and looked deeply into each other's eyes. All those silly things young lovers do before they get married and have kids and have mothers move in with them and wind up in troubling circumstances involving guns and killers and all of those other real life happenings. Finally, after too long, I had my husband back and life was oh, so good. I didn't want the night to end.

We had just finished sharing a melt-in-your mouth tiramisu when Howard drained his second glass of wine and pushed back his chair. "How do you feel about a little disco dancing?"

"I don't know," I said wiping the corners of my mouth with the fancy napkin. "I was thinking less disco, a little more bungle in the jungle." Putting the napkin down, I crossed my arms on the table and bent closer. "I mean, that's alright by me."

"Jethro Tull." He smiled. "Didn't know you were a fan."

"I'm not, but I'm a tiger when I want love."

He pulled a card from his suit jacket pocket and slipped it across the table. "Well, see, I have this invitation..."

The red kissing lips called my name. I picked up the familiar looking card and turned it over. That night's date and the time 9:30 p were scribbled on the back.

"It depends." I fanned myself with the Saturday Night Fever invite. "Will there be dancing tonight...or will there be 'dancing'?"

He leaned in and grinned. The light from the candle on the table reflected in those dark, dreamy eyes. "How about a little of both?"

Now there was an offer I couldn't refuse.

The End

19962374R00107

Made in the USA
Lexington, KY
01 December 2018